CHRISTMAS REDEMPTION

A SMALL TOWN CHRISTIAN ROMANCE

LAURA SCOTT

READSCAPE PUBLISHING, LLC

Copyright © 2020 by Laura Iding

All rights reserved.

No part of this book may be reproduced in any form or by any electronic or mechanical means, including information storage and retrieval systems, without written permission from the author, except for the use of brief quotations in a book review.

❀ Created with Vellum

SWEET ROMANCE READS

As a member of Sweet Romance Reads I invite
you to visit our blog
(https://www.sweetromancereads.com)
to learn more about us and our books.

We are a group of authors who write sweet,
inspirational and/or African-American romances.
We also host our Sweet Romance Cafe on
Facebook which you can find on our website.

Welcome to our world of sweet, clean and
inspirational romance!

**We hope you enjoy our differing approaches to
"Puppies for Christmas."**

1

———

Jack Keller, formerly known as escaped psych patient and prisoner Jesse Kramer, trekked through the woods, following the thin plume of smoke wafting through the trees. When he was close enough to see a log cabin, the obvious source of the smoke, he stopped and pulled his binoculars from his seventy-pound backpack to check it out.

He carried everything he owned in the pack, which wasn't much. Just the barest necessities of what he needed to survive. It had been this way for the past four years as he'd traveled the countryside from central Wisconsin, through upper Michigan into Canada, and back down again.

Even now, a week before Christmas, he wasn't sure why he'd returned to Crystal Lake, Wisconsin. He felt certain the cops were still interested in finding him, so coming back was a risk to his freedom. But his brother Ian was certainly settled down by now, likely with the woman and small boy he'd glimpsed from afar four years ago.

The woman and boy he'd helped rescue from an attempted kidnapping.

One good deed did not make up for the other things he'd done. Jack had no intention of meeting up with his brother, a local sheriff's deputy as of four years ago, since there was no reason to put Ian's job in jeopardy. At this point, he'd be satisfied with watching his brother and his family from afar. For some odd reason, he felt compelled to check on them.

Why, he had no clue. He didn't believe God had brought him here. God hadn't been watching over him for a long time now. He'd covered every mile on his own two feet.

Peering through the binocs, he was surprised to see a woman with long silky dark hair bundled in winter clothing moving outside the cabin. She was pretty and younger than he'd expected to be living in such a remote location. Two dogs, an older German shepherd and a young puppy of the same breed followed her. The puppy in particular was darting around with exuberance as if he or she didn't get out much.

"Belle, sit! Stay!" The woman's voice carried through the quiet woods. "Sadie, watch your puppy, will you? I don't want to step on her."

The puppy let out several barks and sat for all of twenty seconds before bounding up again. The woman shook her head wryly and continued toward the stack of wood cradled between two large trees.

He frowned, wondering where her man was. He couldn't imagine a young woman lived out here alone. Sure, she had dogs, but that wasn't the same as having another human being beside her. Most women he'd known would never stay in a log cabin such as this all by themselves. Women were social creatures by nature.

Not him. Loneliness was his constant companion.

Keeping his binocs trained on the woman, he watched as she picked up a long-handled ax and swung it with the ease of a pro. The blade made a cracking sound when hitting its mark.

What in the world? Why was she chopping her own wood? Especially when there was plenty of wood available on the pile. Was she saving the chopped wood for bad weather? It was what he'd have done, considering the current December weather to date was unusually mild. Lowering his binocs, he considered his next steps. He could make camp here for the night and keep an eye on her, maybe even chop more wood for her. It wouldn't hurt to stick around until her man returned.

Then again, staying far away from people had become second nature. He tried to tell himself this woman and her dogs weren't any of his business. But that didn't stop him from raising the binocs once again.

The woman cut several logs into quarters, then gathered them into her arms. As she headed back toward the cabin, the puppy darted between her feet.

In a nanosecond the woman was down, hitting the ground hard, her pretty facial features twisted in pain.

His heart hammered in his chest, every instinct screaming at him to rush to her side. He forced himself to keep watching, hoping she'd get up and walk without a problem.

Only, she didn't. After several long moments, she began to crawl across the snow-patched ground, pulling herself along on hands and knees with agonizing slowness toward the cabin door.

Without giving himself time to consider the consequences of his actions, Jack shoved the binocs into his backpack and jogged through the woods to where the woman's cabin was located. Being in excellent physical shape, it didn't take him long to reach his destination.

"Grrr." The larger dog came forward, baring her teeth and growling low in her throat. He stopped abruptly, putting his hands in the air so that the dog and the woman would know he wasn't armed.

Even though he was. But only with a knife that was sheathed in his belt. One he wouldn't use except to save his own life.

"Call your dog off," he said, his voice raspy with disuse. "I saw you fall. I'm only here to help."

"Why?" the woman asked, without calling the dog off.

At least she hadn't given the dog a command to attack. "Because you're hurt. I promise I'm not here to cause you harm, I only want to help you inside."

"I'm fine on my own." Her voice was sharp. If she wasn't crawling along the ground, every movement deepening her grimace, he might have believed her. "Just leave me alone. I don't have any money or anything for you to steal."

"I don't want your money or to steal anything. My pack is heavy enough as it is." He knew he looked much like the famed Big Foot, with his bushy beard and shaggy hair. "I only want to help."

"And I told you I'm fine." The words were forced between gritted teeth.

She wasn't fine. He knew it, she knew it. Normally he liked dogs, but Sadie growled with such menace he didn't dare take a step closer.

Ignoring him, the woman hauled herself up onto her knees and reached for the cabin door handle. By some superhuman determination, she managed to get the door open enough to fall inside.

For a moment there was nothing, but then there was movement. When he saw the barrel of a shotgun emerge from the doorway, he smiled for the first time in what seemed like eons.

"Take one step closer and I'll shoot." The woman's voice was clear and strong. "Come, Sadie, Belle."

Belle, the puppy, barked and leaped around like a jumping bean before rushing inside. Sadie stood her ground, growling.

The crooked smile still on his face, he took one step back, then another. Only when he'd put a good ten yards of distance between them did the dog whirl and race inside.

The woman slammed the door shut.

Jack stood for a moment, impressed at the woman's sheer determination to remain independent. To refuse a stranger's offer of help.

He didn't know her name or anything else

about her. Other than she was stubbornly independent.

He deeply admired her for that.

~

RAVEN CLARK LOCKED the cabin door and then let out a low groan.

Her left ankle was on fire from tripping and falling over Belle. As if on cue, the puppy came over and licked her face. "Silly puppy," she muttered. "This is your fault."

Although, really it wasn't. She should have tossed a stick for Belle to chase, her favorite pastime, before hauling the wood inside.

And where on earth had the grizzly bear of a man come from? The way he'd come rushing toward her had about stopped her heart.

Not so much from fear, although she knew better than to let her guard down around strangers, especially big hairy men. More so because she hadn't seen another living soul since a week before Thanksgiving. On her last trip to Crystal Lake, she'd dropped off four Christmas quilts for the consignment shop that displayed her wares. Selling quilts was her main source of income.

After showing off her shotgun, the grizzly bear of a man had backed off, still holding his hands up in the universal gesture of surrender. She almost believed he'd really intended to help.

Almost.

She glanced around the interior of her home for the past five years and figured the grizzly bear guy was smart enough not to risk trying to rob her.

The only thing she had of any value were her dogs, her half-made quilt, and her sewing supplies.

Sadie nudged her, clearly not liking the way Raven was lying on the hardwood floor. The dog had great instincts and was very protective.

"I know, girl. I'm trying." She set the shotgun aside. After dragging herself over to a chair, Raven managed to get up on her hands and knees, then using her uninjured foot, up and into the chair. From there, she shed her thick coat, then unlaced her boots.

Sucking in a harsh breath when her ankle screamed in pain, Raven stared down at the swollen flesh, already beginning to turn darkly bruised.

Not good. She needed to be able to walk around, to care for her dogs, to get wood, and to cook meals.

Sadie came up beside her, whining a little as if knowing things weren't right. She stroked Sadie's soft fur and quelled a sense of panic.

She'd be fine. Granted, having a sprained ankle during winter wasn't optimal, but she'd survived these past sixteen months without Daniel's help, hadn't she? Becoming a widow at the age of thirty had taught her that life wasn't fair. This injury was yet another reminder.

Still, she'd never given up on her faith. No matter what happened, she knew God was watching over her. And He'd continue to watch over her now.

Okay, then. Raven leaned on the table and stood on her right leg, testing her left ankle. Pain shot through her, making her dizzy. Nope, no weight on that foot.

She glanced around the cabin. There was plenty of leftover venison stew, so she wouldn't starve. Unfortunately, there wasn't much firewood inside the cabin, which was why she'd chopped more. It wasn't too cold outside yet, although clouds in the distance hinted at snow. If she turned the woodstove way down, she might have enough to last the night. She could always add a quilt and allow the dogs on her bed for additional warmth.

Eyeing her bin of fabric, she decided wrapping the ankle might provide some stability to the swollen joint.

Using the chair as a makeshift cane, she made her way across the room. Once she'd wrapped her ankle with cheery Christmas fabric, she tried bearing weight on it again, but the pain was still unbearable.

Fine, for now she'd rest and keep her stupid ankle elevated. At least she could still sew, and this was the perfect time to make spring and wedding quilts, two big sellers. The dogs would need to go out again, but she could use the chair for support to accomplish that task.

Tomorrow, she'd crawl outside to get more wood.

See? She'd be okay.

Darkness fell early, and by four thirty in the afternoon, she turned on the lamp closest to her sewing machine and quilt table. So far, she hadn't heard anyone moving around outside, and Sadie hadn't growled in warning, so she felt certain the grizzly bear guy had gone on his merry way.

A good thing, right?

Right. Yet after finishing the section of quilt she'd started, and heating up her stew, she couldn't seem to get him out of her head. Maybe she should have asked for his name and found out what he was doing out here, a good ten miles from the town of Crystal Lake. Maybe he was lost? The thought made her smile. Nah, grizzly guy didn't look like the type to get lost. Tall and muscular with dark blond hair, he lugged that giant pack around like someone who preferred to live off the land.

The way Daniel once had. Before he'd injured himself and had been too stubborn to get treatment until the raging infection had killed him.

She gave herself a mental shake. Why was she thinking about grizzly guy anyway? For all she knew, he was some sort of deep woods serial killer.

After cleaning up the kitchen after dinner, she worked on her quilt to pass the time. When she finished the next square, she decided she may as well let the dogs out and head to bed. The throbbing in her ankle wasn't getting any better, and she was hopeful it would feel better by morning.

"Sadie, Belle, come!" Once again, she dragged the chair with her, leaning on it as she made her way across the cabin toward the door. She eyed Sadie, watching for any sign of nervousness.

Sadie didn't growl, so she felt certain grizzly

guy was long gone. She opened the front door and shooed the dogs out.

Then she saw it. A carved piece of wood leaning up against the wall beside the door. She stared at it for several long moments before reaching for it.

It was the perfect size for her to use as a cane. In fact, the top of the carved piece was made into a ball that she could easily grip in her hand.

Leaning on the handcrafted cane, she swept her gaze over the area, searching for anything amiss.

But even Sadie hadn't barked or growled. Which was strange, as Sadie was an excellent guard dog.

She took another hop-step outside onto the small porch area and noticed the neat stack of chopped wood right beside her door and a small wreath made out of evergreen branches. Everything inside her went still. The logs had been taken from her woodpile and brought up to the cabin, placed within easy reach. And the wreath? Was that some sort of odd gift from grizzly guy?

She raked her gaze over the area again, wondering if he was hiding out nearby or had already left the area for good. Because he had to be the one who'd done this for her.

No one else knew about her injury or lived within ten miles of the cabin. Daniel had chosen this location just for that exact reason.

There was no point in refusing grizzly guy's kind gesture. She carefully carried the wreath inside, then went to work stacking one log at a time inside the cabin. Leaning on the cane was much easier than using the doorframe.

"Thank you," she said in a voice loud enough for him to hear if he was still nearby.

There was no response. But that didn't mean he wasn't out there. In fact, some deeply honed instinct made her believe he was.

But maybe he wasn't a threat. Raven called the dogs in and closed and locked the door behind her.

2

———

J ack smiled and remained in his hiding spot up in a nearby tree long after the pretty woman had gone inside.

Sneaking up to the door with the wind in his face had enabled him to avoid being heard or scented by Sadie. Or from Belle for that matter.

The way she'd stared at the wreath, then thanked him, had warmed his heart. Which was ridiculous as it had been a long time since he'd cared what others thought of him. The past four years he'd learned to live with his demons, but that didn't mean the angry man he'd once been wasn't still lurking deep within.

The only person who mattered to him was his brother, Ian. And this weird sense of urgency to see him again. If he wanted to find his brother soon, he needed to be on his way. From what he remembered, the town was roughly ten miles from here. He hoped Ian was in the same house they'd grown up in, but he knew his brother could have moved.

Except, he couldn't leave the log cabin until

the pretty lady's man came home. If the weather changed—and there was definitely a dampness in the air indicating snow was on the way—she wouldn't be able to manage without help.

After a long hour, Jack came down from the tree and made camp several yards from the cabin. He risked making a small fire, using twigs and branches he found rather than taking anything from the pretty lady's woodpile. In the morning, he'd chop more wood for her so that she'd be all set.

The possibility that she lived here alone, except for the two dogs, bothered him. He'd planned to find his brother before Christmas, but if this woman was truly living here alone, he didn't like leaving her to fend for herself.

What if someone like him came and took advantage of her?

Calling himself all kinds of an idiot, he warmed his hands and feet at the fire. He was running low on food, he hadn't been to a store or hunted for food in over a week, so he made do with jerky from his pack. He didn't have a lot of money, earning what he needed to survive by doing odd jobs when the opportunity presented itself. His last hearty meal had been a wild turkey he'd trapped and roasted over a fire.

He carefully put out the fire before crawling into his tent. Normally closed-in spaces bothered him, but he'd gotten used to the confines of his tent. Sleep never came easily, and tonight was no different. But this time, the problem was that his mind kept going over the brief interaction he'd had with the pretty lady.

After a restless night, he was glad when dawn brightened the horizon. He crawled from his tent, feeling stiff and cold. Even though he was only thirty-four, at times he felt downright ancient. The three years he'd spent deployed overseas was partially responsible, three months of that spent captured and held by Afghani soldiers, but pushing his body to the limit over the past few years hadn't helped either.

Light snowflakes were beginning to fall, so he quickly headed over to the pretty lady's woodpile and began chopping wood. Slinging the ax not only gave him a sense of satisfaction but warmed him up.

When he'd finished chopping the logs that had remained, he ran his hand over his brow and glanced at the cabin, catching a glimpse of movement from inside. Gathering a bunch of freshly cut wood in his arms, he began stacking it outside her door.

This time, he didn't bother to sneak up in an attempt to avoid Sadie, knowing the dog must have already alerted the pretty lady to his presence. And they would have heard him chopping wood. He was surprised by the lack of raucous barking from inside the cabin. Jack told himself that once he'd finished stacking the wood for her, he'd be on his way.

But when he'd returned to the front door with a second load of wood, he stopped abruptly in his tracks. Sitting on the logs he'd just stacked was a cup of coffee and a bowl of what appeared to be oatmeal.

Breakfast. The pretty lady had provided breakfast.

For a few long seconds he couldn't move, unsure of what to do. When it occurred to him that both were growing cold, he quickly set down the logs and picked up the coffee. It was strong and black, the way he liked it.

A smile tugged at the corner of his mouth, a rare occurrence that had now happened three times in less than twenty-four hours. After taking another sip of coffee, he set the mug aside and helped himself to the oatmeal.

It was only lukewarm, but she'd sprinkled brown sugar over the top, which made up for the ambient temperature. He couldn't remember the last time he'd had oatmeal topped with brown sugar.

He ate quickly, then finished the coffee. After carefully setting the cup and bowl aside, he stacked the wood he'd brought over. Then in a loud voice, he called out, "Thank you."

Expecting to hear a muffled *you're welcome*, he was surprised when the front door abruptly opened. He instinctively took a step back, once again holding up his hands so she wouldn't be frightened.

The dogs came bounding outside. The puppy jumped around madly, but he was more concerned about Sadie. He stood still as the German shepherd sniffed him. The dog must have decided he wasn't a threat because she took off with the puppy, racing around to do their business.

He looked at the pretty lady. She didn't have the shotgun this time, which meant she'd gotten past seeing him as an enemy. He felt bad about that, since at one time he'd been very much an enemy to those around him. "Thank you for breakfast," he said, his voice low and husky.

"It's the least I could do." She leaned on the cane he'd crafted for her, her head tilted to one side. "Why did you do all this?"

He didn't understand the question. "Why wouldn't I? You're hurt, and I don't see your man anywhere around."

Her eyebrow levered upward. "You think I'm helpless?"

"No. Sadie and the pup would both protect you. And you clearly have a shotgun. I just hope you're not afraid to use it."

"I'm not." She continued staring at him curiously. "Who are you?"

Her question knocked him back a step. "J-Jack Keller." He'd almost slipped up and given her his real name. "I'm just passing through."

"I'm Raven Clark." She stared at him. "You know the Crystal Lake area?"

"It's been a long time." He was humbled she'd given him her name. Raven. It was perfect for her, the color of a raven the exact same hue as her dark silky hair.

He was irritated with himself for noticing.

"Well, thanks again for chopping wood, the cane, and the wreath." Her mention of the foolishly sentimental gift made his ears burn. "I appreciate your help, Jack, but it's not necessary. I'm fine, truly."

"Okay." He couldn't argue, after all, she appeared very comfortable living out here. "Again, thanks for breakfast."

"Take care." The snow picked up, coming down fast enough that the flakes stuck to the dog's fur like an additional layer as they came running back.

He turned away, hunching his shoulders as snowflakes slipped down the back of his neck. He heard Raven call the dogs in and the door close behind him. He finished stacking the wood, then closed the distance to where he'd left his pack. He considered hiking out toward Crystal Lake, but the way the snow was coming down made him realize he'd be better off to stay put. Hiking in a snowstorm was hardly smart.

With economical movements, he put up his small tent. It would be a long day waiting out the storm, but he was accustomed to it. Maybe he'd catch up on the sleep he'd missed the previous night.

The wind picked up, battering his tent. He hunkered down in his sleeping bag, listening to the storm. It wasn't the first and wouldn't be the last.

"Jack? Jack, can you hear me?"

He blinked, wondering if he was dreaming. Then he heard Sadie's deep bark, followed by another, "Jack!"

It took a moment to shimmy out of the sleeping bag. He opened the tent zipper and peered out. Raven was hobbling across the snow with her cane.

Was she crazy coming outside like that? What if she fell again? Moving quickly, he emerged from the tent and came toward her. "What are you doing?"

"You can't sleep out here in the storm," she shouted, the wind whipping around them. "Come inside."

He stared dumbly at her for a moment. She shouldn't invite him inside when she didn't know the first thing about him. About the broken man he'd once been.

Might still be.

But then she wobbled, nearly toppling over. With a sigh, he lurched forward and scooped her into his arms. Ignoring Sadie's and Belle's barking and racing around him, he carried her into the cabin.

"I—what?" she sputtered.

He set Raven on the chair closest to the door. Then, when he realized she'd dropped her cane, he went back out to retrieve it. The dogs crowded around her, licking the snow from her clothes.

"You shouldn't have come outside in that weather," he scolded lightly. "You almost fell again."

"What were you thinking to sleep outside in the middle of a blizzard?" she shot back. "You'll freeze to death out there."

The corner of his mouth kicked up in a reluctant smile. Her concern was sweet. Misplaced, but sweet. "Where do you think I've been sleeping over the past few years? I have excellent cold-weather gear."

"Years?" She gaped at him.

He ran a self-conscious hand over his bushy beard. He tried to think back to the last time he'd stayed in a motel. Must have been over a year ago. "Pretty much."

She flushed. "You must think I'm an idiot."

It wouldn't behoove him to agree. "You're too kind, that's all. But rest assured I would never hurt you." He turned toward the door.

"Wait." The hint of panic in her voice had him turning to face her. "I can't stand the idea of you sleeping out there. Please, just stay inside for a while. Once the storm blows over, you can be on your way."

Now it was his turn to gape. "Why do you trust me?"

She lifted a shoulder. "No one has ever made a wreath, a cane, and chopped wood for me." Her smile was lopsided. "I decided you probably aren't a deep woods serial killer."

The urge to laugh was strong, and something he hadn't done in years. "I'm not."

"So you'll stay? Otherwise, I'll feel compelled to bring food out to you."

And she would too. The stubborn glint was back in her clear blue eyes, and he sensed nothing stopped Raven from what she wanted to do.

Even him.

"I'll stay." The words came out slowly. "On one condition."

She tensed. "What?"

He fingered his beard again. "Will you allow me to use your shower and borrow clippers to clean up a bit? I'm sure I don't smell too good. It's been months since I was in a campground with running water."

Her blue gaze clung to his for a long moment.

"Of course, there's a shaving kit complete with clippers in the bathroom closet. Help yourself."

"Thanks." He went outside long enough to take down his tent and bring in his pack. He locked the door and checked the wood-burning stove to be sure it didn't need additional wood. Satisfied all was in order, he carried his pack over to the small bathroom.

His image in the mirror was worse than he'd imagined. He told himself cleaning up was the least he could do. He didn't want Raven to regret inviting him in for a brief stay.

Yet, deep down, he knew that this was the first time in four years he'd cared enough to look presentable for anyone.

Especially a woman.

~

RAVEN BUSIED herself in the kitchen, cleaning up the breakfast dishes while Jack used her shower. She was shocked he'd asked for clippers. From all appearances, he hadn't used one in a long time.

What had he said? Months since he stayed in a campground with running water?

Impossible to imagine. Her cabin was remote, but she had running water, electricity, and even a generator if the power went out.

Letting Jack Keller stay in her house had seemed like a good idea at the time, but a sliver of doubt had crept into her mind. Okay, he probably wasn't a deep woods serial killer, but that didn't mean he didn't have other nefarious plans in mind.

Except—she didn't think so. She'd always trusted her gut, and right now her instincts were telling her there was no reason to be afraid. She glanced at the wreath she'd hung on the kitchen wall. As far as she knew, Jack the Ripper hadn't spent time creating a wreath for his victims.

Using the cane for support, she made another pot of coffee. Rummaging in her fridge, she found a block of cheddar cheese. She had homemade bread from yesterday and decided she could offer to make grilled cheese sandwiches for lunch.

And wasn't she a good hostess?

With a wry groan, she closed the fridge and dropped into a kitchen chair, realizing she felt nervous about sharing her space with Jack. Other than infrequent trips to Crystal Lake to get supplies and sell her quilts, she didn't mingle with people. Even when she'd sold Sadie's last litter of puppies just ten weeks ago, all except for a last-minute decision to keep Belle, her customers stayed outside in the front yard.

When was the last time she'd had someone inside her home? Probably not since Daniel died.

Was this a mistake? A glance at the window confirmed the snow was still coming down at a fast clip. Already her woodpile was covered in a thick layer of glistening white snow.

After filling her cup with coffee, she sat at the table with her ankle up on a pillow while waiting for Jack to appear. He was gone for what seemed like a really long time, and when he emerged with a neatly trimmed beard, wearing clean clothes, his damp hair tied back from his face, she hardly recognized him.

Had his hair always been so blond? His eyes so green?

"Coffee?" The hope in the single word made her smile.

"Help yourself." She couldn't seem to tear her gaze from him. "You look—very different."

He idly rubbed a hand over his closely cropped bearded cheek. "I'll probably regret this when I head out later this afternoon, a full beard helps keep my face warm."

She frowned. "Then why on earth did you trim it so close?"

With a shrug, he padded over to the coffeepot. He filled his cup, then came over to the table to sit across from her. She wondered if he was keeping a respectful distance on purpose to avoid scaring her or if he just naturally avoided people.

She suspected the latter.

"I figured I'd look less scary." He sipped the coffee. "Thanks, this is great."

"It's just coffee." She tried to hide the strange flash of awareness that hit her between the eyes. She looked away to hide her reaction. "I hope you don't mind grilled cheese sandwiches for lunch and leftover venison stew for dinner."

"Venison stew?" He looked surprised. "Your husband shot a deer this season?"

The way he referred to her man, her husband, her whatever was beginning to annoy her. "I killed the deer. Gutted it and dragged it back here. Cut it up and gave some to the townsfolk in Crystal Lake in exchange for flour and yeast." She wasn't going to add that it was the hardest thing she'd ever done and wasn't all that keen on doing again.

"You did that?" He looked as if she'd told him she'd climbed Mount Everest one-handed. "By yourself?"

"Yes, all by myself." She stared at her swollen ankle for a long moment. "I've been trying to tell you I'm fine here alone. Have been fine for the past sixteen months since my husband died."

A long silence hung between them. Finally, he said, "I'm sorry for your loss."

"Me too," she said simply. "But as you can see, I'm pretty self-sufficient. Once the storm blows over, you should head to Crystal Lake. They have a motel if you need a place to stay."

He nodded and drank his coffee as if savoring every sip. "I haven't been back to Crystal Lake in four years." His blunt statement broke the silence.

"Oh? And why is that?"

He didn't answer for so long, Raven figured he planned to ignore her question. She shouldn't have pushed. He didn't seem the type to share anything personal about himself.

Normally, she didn't either. So why had she blabbed about being a widow?

No clue.

"I had some personal problems from my last military deployment overseas," Jack said slowly. "Those issues made it difficult for me to be around people."

She knew he was talking about post-traumatic stress disorder, a common ailment for those who served in combat. Her heart went out to him, unable to imagine what he must have been through.

"I can understand that," she said softly. When

he looked up at her, she caught the flash of gratitude in his green eyes.

Her heart thumped erratically in her chest.

Oh boy. This wasn't good. It was one thing to
have Jack wait out the storm here inside the cabin.

But it would be a big mistake to let her guard
down long enough to like him.

3

———

Raven was a widow. The stunning revelation made him glad he hadn't left her to fend for herself with a bum ankle. Still, the news made him even more surprised that she'd been brave enough to invite him in. Good thing she didn't know his past history here, or she would have called the cops instead.

The way Sadie stood beside Raven, he felt certain that if Raven told the shepherd to attack, she would. He figured between the shotgun and guard dog, Raven could hold her own.

The puppy, on the other hand, tugged on the edge of his flannel shirt playfully, darting around with an abundance of energy. For a moment his past darkened his gaze, but he ruthlessly shoved it aside. "Hey, Belle," he said, lowering his hand so the puppy could give him a good sniff. "You're cute."

"She needs a firm hand," Raven corrected, gesturing to her swollen ankle with a sigh. "Obviously, I need to do a better job training her."

"Speaking of which, I'd like to take a look at

your ankle, if you don't mind." His voice still sounded a bit hoarse; he hadn't spoken this much in years.

"Do you have medical training?"

For a moment, his mind flashed to the explosion that had taken out half his team. Screams echoed around him as he struggled to make his way through the debris to reach his injured men. When he'd found them, he'd known it was too late, but he couldn't leave. He could still see his best friend Freddie's empty gaze.

Freddie!

"Jack?"

Raven's voice pulled him back to the present. He blinked, then slowly shook his head, desperately searching for the thread of their conversation. "No formal training." Just what he'd learned on the battlefield.

"It's fine, really. I used an ice pack last night, and the swelling isn't any worse." Raven's blue eyes held a gentle understanding that made him desperate to change the subject.

He didn't share his flashbacks or his experience in captivity with anyone.

So why was he here, talking to her? He gave himself a mental shake. Time to get back on track. "Ice on for twenty minutes, then heat for twenty minutes. We'll start with ice." He rose and walked to the fridge, Belle on his heels. "Sit," he said sternly. The puppy sat. "Good girl."

He could feel Raven's gaze on him as he removed the ice pack from the freezer and brought it over to wrap the cold pack around her swollen joint. The way she'd placed Christmas fabric around her ankle made him want to smile. He held the pack in place until it warmed enough to conform to her injured joint.

When Belle leaped up, he turned and pointed to the floor again. "Sit."

Once again, Belle sat.

"She thinks you're the alpha dog," Raven said with a wry smile as he stepped away, leaving the ice pack in place.

He nodded. "I am, yes. I can work with her a bit while you rest."

Raven considered his offer. "Okay, but she has to listen to me too once you're gone."

"We'll practice with you too. Like this." He took several steps away from the kitchen table and said, "Come, Belle."

The puppy bounded toward him, jumping up in an attempt to lick him.

"Sit," he commanded again.

Belle sat, and he lavished her with praise. Then he looked at Raven and nodded.

"Come, Belle," Raven said.

The puppy whirled and ran back to Raven, making her laugh. Jack absorbed the sound of Raven's laughter like a dying man drinking from the river.

He hadn't felt connected to another human being, other than his brother Ian, in a very long time.

Since returning from his final tour in Afghanistan.

He told himself that Raven wasn't looking for a connection to him, likely still grieving for her husband. But that was okay.

Even knowing this was temporary, he'd be content with anything she chose to share with him.

He'd be back out on his own soon enough.

RAVEN COULDN'T REMEMBER when she'd enjoyed a morning more. Training Belle with Jack's help was fun and provided another reason to be grateful to him.

The fact that he was extremely easy on the eyes didn't hurt either. Normally, she didn't like long hair on men, but Jack's rugged features carried it off in a way that most men couldn't.

She averted her gaze, feeling foolish. Jack was a wounded warrior and not the type to stay in one place for long. Any man who'd sleep in a tent in the middle of a blizzard didn't need a home.

And she wasn't offering one anyway.

Except as a shelter for a few hours, until the storm passed.

An exhausted Belle slept curled in Jack's lap, looking as if she belonged there. He glanced at the wood-burning stove, and she knew he was hesitant to disturb the puppy to feed the fire.

Easing her leg off the seat of the chair, she reached for her cane. In a flash, Jack was on his feet, cradling the puppy with one large hand. "Where are you going?"

"I need to add wood to the fire and begin making lunch." He acted as if she hadn't taken care of herself over the past twenty-four hours since injuring her ankle. "I can manage."

"But you don't have to." Laying a hand on her shoulder, he gently pushed her back down and set Belle in her lap as an added measure to keep her seated. "I'll take care of the chores."

"It's my house," she protested, stroking Belle's soft fur. The puppy snuggled closer.

He didn't answer, first stoking the wood-burning stove, then padding back into the kitchen. "I can make the grilled cheese sandwiches."

Of course he could, she figured Jack could do anything he set his mind to. Since arguing appeared to be fruitless, she let him cut the cheese and slice the bread as butter melted in the fry pan.

As he cooked, it occurred to her that she had no idea what they would do for the rest of the day. A quick glance outside proved the snow hadn't let up one iota; in fact, everything was covered in at least three inches of snow.

If this kept up, they'd have a solid foot before nightfall.

Until today, the snow had been negligible, the temperatures on the mild side. Welcome to winter in the north woods of Wisconsin.

"I, uh, have some sewing to do," she said, breaking the silence. "There's a small washer and dryer combo if you're interested in washing your things."

Jack shot her a look over his shoulder. "I'd appreciate that, thanks. Tell me about your sewing."

She shifted on the chair. "There's nothing to tell. I make quilts; they sell fairly well in Crystal Lake's craft shop."

"Nice." He hesitated, then asked, "Is that how you earn a living?"

"That and selling Sadie's pups. I only breed her once a year though. I don't want to wear her out."

"Belle was from her recent litter?"

"Yes." She hesitated, glancing down at the puppy. "I decided at the last minute that Belle could take Sadie's place in a couple of years. I wouldn't necessarily breed her at all, except that the money pays my property taxes."

He nodded slowly. "Understandable. I'm sure Sadie's pups are in high demand."

She flushed, thinking of the last encounter she'd had with buyers for the puppies. Most of the time things went well, but once in a while, they didn't. But she wasn't going to bother Jack with her issues. "Yes, I guess the word has gotten out because I already have a waiting list for the next litter. I used to get specific requests about males versus females, but now people are saying they'll take whatever is available."

Jack looked down at Sadie. "She has quite the reputation."

"She does and so does the sire of this recent litter, Duke. He's even better trained than Sadie." She stroked Sadie behind the ears. "I'm thankful to have her."

Jack froze for a moment, and she wondered if she'd said something wrong. But he seemed to collect himself. After grilling their sandwiches, he brought the plates to the table, setting one in front of her and returning to his seat across from her with the other. She bowed her head and silently thanked God for the food Jack had prepared for them to eat and for guiding her on the right path. She added another prayer for God to help heal Jack. When she opened her eyes, she was all too aware of Jack sitting stock-still, his gaze downcast as he waited for her to finish.

She wanted to stay something, to remind Jack that God was still there watching over him, despite his terrible experiences, but she was afraid any such attempt would only alienate him.

Selfishly, she didn't want him to leave until the snow stopped. She couldn't bear the thought of him sleeping in the snow with nothing but his tent for protection. Logically, she knew he was used to it, but still, the idea bothered her.

There was a long silence as they ate.

"Any particular reason you're heading to Crystal Lake?" She glanced at him curiously. "Do you have family in the area?"

A startled expression flashed in his green eyes, before he looked away. It was a long moment before he replied in a low voice, "My brother."

She couldn't remember anyone with the last name of Keller, but then again, she didn't know many of the townsfolk by name. She knew Josie who ran Rose's Café, Carla the woman who ran the Crystal Lake craft shop, and Hank who ran Billy's Auto Repair. The townsfolk didn't like changing the names of their businesses even though both Billy and Rose were long gone. Hank's mechanic Brian did a lot of work on her truck, although next time, she'd ask Hank for someone else. Brian had acted a little strange.

"I'm sure your brother will be thrilled to have

you home for Christmas." She frowned. "Will he worry if you don't show up by a certain day and time?"

Jack avoided her gaze, eating his sandwich methodically. "No, he won't worry."

Noting his empty plate, she waved a hand toward the stove. "Go ahead and make yourself another sandwich. There's plenty of bread and cheese."

He sat still for a long moment, before lifting his eyes to meet hers. "I would like to offer you something in return for your kindness. Are there additional chores you need completed?"

"In a blizzard? No. I was thinking of raising chickens starting in the spring, but I haven't gotten as far as making a chicken coop." She flushed when she realized how that might sound as if she was fishing for his help. "Not that I'm asking you to make one, that wouldn't be possible to do in the middle of winter anyway."

He nodded slowly. "I can see the value of raising chickens, especially having fresh eggs. But you'd need to run electric out there to keep them warm in the winter."

"I know. That's why I haven't started that project yet." It had been on Daniel's list of things he'd wanted to do but hadn't accomplished before he died. "Honestly, I'm set for now, just go ahead and wash your clothes."

Jack stood and went to make another sandwich. "I'll clean up the kitchen when I've finished eating, then borrow your washer. I'll also bring the rest of the wood inside and let the dogs out."

"Don't sit still much, do you?" She moved her

injured ankle off the chair and used the cane he'd crafted for her to stand. The joint still hurt, but not as badly as yesterday. She thought she could hobble over to the far corner of the living room where her sewing machine and quilt table were set up.

She'd only made it two steps before Jack noticed. With a scowl, he quickly lifted her in his arms again, just like he had earlier to bring her inside.

"You can't keep carrying me around," she protested.

He ignored her comment, setting her down in front of the sewing machine. "The cane isn't great when it comes to keeping weight off your foot. I would have made crutches, but I didn't have enough time."

She felt self-conscious at how he'd twice picked her up as though she didn't weigh more than a feather, which she knew was not true. "Don't you have to measure crutches?"

The corner of his mouth twitched in a semblance of a smile. "There is that. I estimated the size of the cane based on how tall you were compared to the side of the cabin. Not sure if that would have worked as well for crutches."

"Did you now?" She picked through her bin of fabric for what she was looking for, then glanced up at him. "Guess that means you were watching me for a while."

He flushed and backed away. "Not long, just enough to see you chop wood, then trip over Belle."

"Hmm." The news that he'd watched her for

that length of time should have annoyed her but didn't. Instead, she tried to understand who Jack Keller really was.

A knight in tarnished armor? Maybe.

She turned her attention to her sewing but was keenly aware of Jack moving around the cabin. It wasn't until he took the dogs outside for a bathroom break that she took a deep breath and let it out slowly.

It had only been a few hours since she'd convinced him to seek shelter inside. Yet it seemed as if he belonged here.

Which was far from the truth. She needed to get a grip on her crazy emotions. Just because he'd taken the time to make a wreath and a cane didn't mean anything. Other than he was a nice guy.

It wouldn't be smart to read into his kind gestures. Especially since she suspected that he'd only done that as an attempt to allay her fears.

She concentrated on her sewing. The snow would stop eventually, and Jack would be on his way. She'd pray for his safety while letting him go without complaint.

And that's exactly the way it should be.

JACK USED his boot to shove snow aside for Belle. The poor thing was trying her best to maneuver in the deep snow, but she wasn't quite tall enough to get around the way Sadie had.

He took a deep breath of the fresh air. Despite the fact that he lived in his tent more often than not, sharing the cabin with Raven was proving to be more difficult than he'd anticipated.

Not just because it was an enclosed space, his severe claustrophobia had gotten better over time. It was the way her scent lingered everywhere and clouded his judgment. If he were smart, he'd wait until Raven retired to her bedroom for the night, then scoot outside to sleep in his tent.

Too bad he wasn't that smart.

Sadie began to growl low in her throat. Without hesitation, he picked up Belle and rested his hand on the knife sheathed in his belt. He didn't like to use it but would do so as a means to protect himself.

And the innocent, like Raven.

He should have checked the perimeter of the cabin long before now, more proof that he was losing his edge. He'd come in from the northeast. Now, moving in the opposite direction, he was surprised to find a decent-sized garage. Logically, it made sense that Raven would have a vehicle, hadn't she mentioned going into town to sell her quilts? She wouldn't be able to walk ten miles carrying them, that's for sure.

The area behind the garage had been cleared away, maybe for the chicken coop she'd mentioned. It made him feel bad he wouldn't be there to help her get the coop up and running, but he'd be long gone by the time the weather turned nice.

He never stayed in one place for longer than a few days.

Sadie's growls deepened, and he felt certain there was some sort of wildlife back there that had gotten her attention. Maybe a cougar or a wolf. He'd gotten a glimpse of a cougar a few days ago, several miles north of here. He hadn't minded watching it from afar.

But if the animal was this close, he wished he'd grabbed Raven's shotgun.

"Easy, Sadie," he murmured. He'd have to mention the threat of cougars to Raven in case she did put up a chicken coop.

A fox wasn't the only threat to a henhouse. Cougars, coyotes, and other wild animals looking for their next easy meal would stake the place out too.

Still cradling Belle in his arms, Jack lowered himself to his haunches to look for tracks on the snow-covered ground. He'd seen a lot of deer and turkey over the past few days, and of course the cougar.

He frowned as he noticed something strange. Moving cautiously, he approached the area between the garage and the cabin.

There were tracks in the snow all right, but these didn't belong to an animal.

Not the four-legged kind.

These were human tracks. They weren't his, since he hadn't come this way.

They belonged to someone else. Someone who'd clearly lurked outside Raven's cabin.

4

———

Raven tried not to turn around when Jack and the dogs returned. She continued working on her square, using the yellow and blue flowered print she'd chosen as the main design for this particular quilt.

She shivered as Jack brought several loads of wood inside before closing and locking the cabin door. Finally, when she couldn't stand it another second, she glanced over her shoulder at him.

The grim expression on his face sent a warning shiver down her spine. "What's wrong?"

He reached up to wipe melted snow from his beard. "Have you had anyone bothering you lately?"

She lifted a brow. "Besides you?"

He didn't smile, which only added to her level of concern. "Yes, besides me."

"No, why?" She glanced outside at the snow still coming down. "Did you see someone?"

"Not exactly." He unlaced his boots and removed them, then came toward her, his gaze narrowing at the double window over her sofa. "You sit here often?"

His questions were beginning to annoy her. "Only when I'm working." Which was every single day. "Why? Tell me what's going on."

He leaned over her shoulder and peered out the window. His woodsy scent made her mouth go dry. "I saw some footprints in the snow."

She glanced up with a frown. "How do you know they're not yours or mine?"

"Not mine because I was never on this side of the cabin. Didn't even realize you had a garage over here. And not yours because they're too big."

"A man?" She struggled to stand, but he held her in place with a hand on her shoulder. "You think there was a man out there? In the middle of a storm? Who would do something like that? Other than you," she hastened to add.

"I don't know, that's why I'm asking if anyone has been bothering you lately." His hand was warm on her shoulder, and she wondered if he'd forgotten it was there. "What about when you were in town to drop off your quilts? Anyone bother you then?"

"No. I dropped off my quilts, took the money I made to do some grocery shopping, and had my car tuned up in Billy's garage." She stared out the window, wondering if this was something he'd made up just to scare her. It didn't seem to fit his character, but what did she really know about Jack Keller?

He was kind enough to make a wreath, a cane, and move her wood. No way would he make up a story to scare her on purpose.

"Keep the dogs inside with you, I'm heading back out for a few minutes." He lifted his hand from her shoulder, and she instantly missed the warmth. "I'll take a look around the property, see if I can figure out if this was just some lost soul or what."

Lost soul was how she would have described Jack, but he suddenly looked every bit the warrior he'd been. She noticed he picked up her shotgun. And then there was a large knife in his hand.

"You have a knife?" Her voice came out in a squeak.

There was a glimmer of hurt and reproach in his green gaze. "I promise not to hurt you, or anyone else except in self-defense."

Before she could respond to that, he stuffed his feet back into his boots and quickly laced them up. In the blink of an eye, he was outside again, closing the cabin door behind him.

The abrupt silence inside the cabin was disturbing. Which was strange as the quietness never bothered her before.

She told herself a knife was critical to surviving in the woods. And it wasn't a gun.

Would he tell her he had a gun? Maybe not. Then again, he'd taken her shotgun, making her think he didn't have one of his own.

"Sadie, come." Her shepherd immediately came to her side, nuzzling her hand. Belle bounced over too, going up on her hind legs indicating she wanted to be in her lap.

Snuggling the puppy and her protector close, she waited.

And prayed that God would watch over Jack.

~

JACK MELTED into the shadows with the ease of long practice. He was an expert at navigating the wilderness without detection. However, being out in the snow was a problem on several levels. It was easier to see people moving against the white backdrop, unless one was wearing white camouflage, which he wasn't. And there was the problem of leaving footprints in the snow, which would be difficult to cover up considering there was a good six inches down already, with more to come.

Still, the intruder had the same disadvantages he did, and he doubted the guy possessed his level of skill.

Not that Jack planned to underestimate him.

Why had this guy come here? If he'd wanted to target Raven, why wait until the middle of a snowstorm? It made Jack's blood run cold to imagine him spying on Raven.

He found the intruder's footprints and crouched down to see them more clearly. Risking the flashlight, he shined the beam on the interior of the footprint, measuring it against his own. Smaller, but only by two inches, so likely belonging to a man.

Raven's feet were small, barely a size seven, and she hadn't been out here since coming to rouse him from his tent. The indentation made by the boot was already filling with fresh snow. Measuring what had already fallen, Jack knew they were seeing an inch of snow per hour.

Less than a half inch filled the footprint. The

intruder had been here roughly thirty minutes ago.

Turning off the flashlight, he continued following the footprints while being careful not to interfere with them. It didn't take long for him to find the path this guy had taken. He'd likely started from the road where there were fresh tire tracks, coming through the woods and up to the cabin, then away again.

The road was about a half mile from the cabin. The intruder had made the hike in deep snow there and back, indicating he was in decent shape.

But what bothered Jack was not just why this guy had decided to show up today in a snowstorm, but how? How had the intruder known the location of Raven's cabin? Because he'd been there before? If so, when?

He didn't know, and he didn't like it.

Kneeling beside the tire tracks, he scowled when he realized he must have just missed the guy by fifteen minutes. The tire tracks were also wide and deeply grooved, likely a truck of some sort. It made sense—a car wasn't going to make it through deep snow without a strong possibility of getting stuck. He knew most people living in the north preferred four-wheel drive.

Based on the snow, it was a good choice.

Broadening his search area, Jack made sure there were no other human footprints that he may have missed.

He didn't find anything else. Whoever the intruder was, he must have been scared off when he saw Jack through the windows or heard Jack come out with the dogs.

After stomping snow off his boots on the porch, he headed back inside.

"You didn't have the door locked," he scolded.

"You don't have a key," Raven pointed out. "Besides, I highly doubt anyone would get past you."

Her faith in him was humbling, especially since they'd only spoken to each other for the first time earlier that morning. It was unnerving to feel as if he'd known her for weeks, rather than hours.

"I followed the footprints in the snow from the southwest side of the house to the road and back." After shucking his winter clothes, he crossed over to sit beside her on the edge of the sofa located near her sewing machine. "Whoever was out there knew some details about your property."

Raven finished a seam, then stopped the machine and turned to face him. "Until today, I haven't had guests here since Daniel died."

"But you did have people come to pick up their puppies, right?"

She frowned. "Yes."

He waited, hoping she'd fill him in, but she didn't. Instead, she had a faraway look in her eyes, as if she were remembering something.

"What is it?" he pressed.

She sighed and reluctantly met his gaze. "There was . . . an incident with one of the clients who came to pick up his puppy."

He tensed and leaned forward. "What kind of incident?"

"This guy, Taylor Wilkes, never smiled and seemed, I don't know, kinda mean. He used his foot to push one of the other puppies out of the way." She shrugged and met his gaze. "He didn't hurt the pup, but I didn't like it."

He could understand her reaction. If he'd have been there, he might have flattened the guy. "What happened?"

Raven gestured at Belle. "I told him I changed my mind and needed to keep Belle for myself because I was worried about her having health problems. I gave him his money back, but he wasn't happy. Demanded I make good on our deal. I stayed firm, and he eventually left."

He found himself growing angry on her behalf. "When was this?"

"Four weeks ago now." She hesitated, then added, "I wasn't completely honest with him about the health problems. Belle is fine."

"Do you have other identifying information about him, like his address and phone number?"

"Yes, but you can't assume that Taylor is the guy who left those footprints," she protested. "They could belong to anyone."

"They could, but unless you know of anyone else who might be upset with you, he's at the top of my suspect list."

She snorted. "You're a cop now?"

"No." In fact, he'd been on the wrong end of the law in the past. Back when he'd been in a dark place. He'd been shocked and horrified to learn Belle's sire was Duke, the dog he'd threatened to harm.

Pulling his thoughts to the present, he focused on the fact that he knew a cop. His brother Ian and a few of the other deputies within the sheriff's department. By the time they came out here, the prints would be filled with fresh snow. As would the tire tracks along the edge of the road.

No proof, but it would still be a good idea for Raven to file a complaint. Having a paper trail, especially if he returned, would be important.

The biggest problem he had would be Raven herself. No way was he leaving her alone with a bad ankle while this guy was still out there somewhere. He was staying until this guy was caught.

A decision he was sure Raven wouldn't take very well.

~

RAVEN TORE her gaze from Jack to stare blindly outside. He'd seen footprints in the snow that went to the road. That didn't mean Taylor had come back to do—what exactly? Force her at gunpoint to give up Belle?

Ridiculous. For one thing, he would know Sadie would protect her. And really, the guy could get a dog anywhere. While she chose the pups' sire carefully, using Reese Webber's well-trained Duke for her last litter, there were plenty of other people out there breeding dogs. Duke had sired several litters.

"Raven?"

Hearing her name in Jack's low husky voice sent shivers down her spine. Really, she needed to get a grip. The guy was only here because she'd been silly enough to worry about him sleeping in his tent. She pulled herself together and looked at him. "Yes?"

His green gaze was intense. "You looked as if you were far away for a moment. The intruder is likely this Wilkes guy, isn't it?"

"It seems a little crazy, but he's the only one I can think of that has been upset with me recently." She thought for a moment about how Brian had leered at her while fixing her truck but brushed it off. Likely just his way of being friendly.

It was her fault, she'd long forgotten how to be friendly with strangers.

"Recently?" It took her a moment to realize Jack had capitalized on her comment. "What about not so recently?"

She waved a hand in frustration. "You're making a big deal out of nothing. For all we know, someone had some car trouble, walked up to the cabin, then got a glimpse of you and figured they'd be safer calling for a tow truck than asking for a favor."

He didn't smile, the way she'd hoped. "This is serious, Raven. Tell me who else might be holding a grudge against you."

"There's only one other person who might have a reason to be upset with me," she said. "But I barely know the guy."

"Who?" Jack's voice was dangerously soft.

She didn't like looking for boogeymen around every corner, but Jack was worse than a dog with a bone. "Sean Calloway. He's older, maybe in his late forties, early fifties and was selling his wood carvings in the same consignment shop that sells my quilts."

"Go on," Jack said when she paused.

"I guess my quilts were doing better for Carla, so she told Sean that she wasn't going to carry his woodworking any longer." She shrugged. "According to Carla, he said some nasty things about me before sweeping up his carvings and stomping out of there."

"And when did you hear about that?" Jack pressed.

"The last time I was in town, the week before Thanksgiving is when Carla told me, but I think she kicked him out at the beginning of November." She stared gloomily at her ankle. "Again, why would he come after me? I'd think Carla would be a better target. She made the decision to offer more shelf space to my quilts, not me."

"Except that striking back at Carla doesn't get him what he wants, which is sales. With your quilts out of the way, he could easily display his woodworking in Carla's shop, hoping to make back some of the revenue he'd lost." Jack stared at her thoughtfully. "Another good suspect."

She rolled her eyes. "Seriously, Jack, I can't imagine either one of these guys coming out here in the middle of a snowstorm to find me. It doesn't make any sense."

"It only has to make sense in their minds, not ours." Jack sat quietly for several minutes before rising to his feet. "I need to get my laundry."

She turned back to her quilting, realizing she hadn't been nearly as productive as usual. Peering closer, she noticed the seam was crooked. Frustrated with her inattentiveness, she picked out the crooked seam to start over.

If Jack didn't get out of her house and her hair

soon, she'd never finish this quilt. And she needed a nice stockpile for spring.

Forcing herself to concentrate, she completed another quilt square, barely glancing over as Jack came out of the kitchen, then disappeared back down the hallway.

After an hour, she straightened, rubbing the back of her neck. She'd finally made a little progress. Shifting around in her seat, she reached for the cane and stood.

Jack came into the room as if he'd been alerted by some sort of motion sensor. "What do you need, Raven?"

"To move, I've been sitting for too long." She wasn't about to tell him she needed to use the bathroom. Honestly, the guy hovered worse than a mother hen.

When he took a step toward her, she leaned on her cane and held up her hand. "No. You can't keep carrying me around, Jack."

He eyed her warily. "Why not?"

She flushed and hoped he didn't notice. "Because it's not right." Schooling her features so she wouldn't grimace, she hobbled toward the bathroom.

Seconds later, she was back in Jack's arms. Without saying a word, he carried her into the bathroom and then set her down on the commode. "You're very stubborn."

"And you're not?"

This time, she was rewarded with a half-smile. "I think it's what I admire the most about you."

He left, closing the door behind him. Stunned speechless, she glanced around, expecting to see a mess from when he'd showered and trimmed his beard.

The room was spotless. She scowled. It wasn't normal. He wasn't normal. There wasn't a man on the planet that was this neat and tidy.

Maybe he wasn't a man at all, but an alien. Yeah, that was it. He was something she'd conjured from a dream of the perfect man.

Shaking her head at her foolishness, she used the bathroom, then spent a few minutes tidying her hair.

The minute she opened the door, Jack was standing there. She was surprised to see a screwdriver in his hand.

"Are you going to stab me if I don't let you carry me around anymore?"

Again, the corner of his mouth tipped up in a smile. "No, I just finished fixing your washing machine."

"Fix it? There was nothing wrong with it!" Was he one of those men who felt the need to take things apart for no reason? If so, they were going to have a problem.

"You didn't hear the thumping noise the drum made on the spin cycle?"

She pursed her lips. "Maybe."

He scooped her into his arms and carried her back into the main living space. "Sofa, sewing machine, or kitchen?"

Her face was so close to his, she could see he'd nicked himself while trimming his golden beard. His mouth was firm, and it took every ounce of her willpower to tear her gaze away. "Kitchen," she managed. "It's almost time for dinner."

"I have the venison stew warming on the stove." He carried her into the kitchen and set her on the chair. "Comfy?"

She nodded, unable to speak. But the truth was, the chair wasn't nearly as good as being carried in his arms.

Which was her problem, not his. All she needed to do was to control her crazy emotions until the storm passed.

Before she did something really out of character. Like give in to the urge to kiss him.

5

Jack focused on stirring the venison stew, the scent made his mouth water, but it wasn't easy to get the image of Raven's sweet face out of his mind.

He couldn't allow himself to get attached to her. For her sake, not his. Sure, he felt better now than he had four years ago, tolerating people without getting angry. Even being in her log cabin wasn't as bad as he'd imagined. But Raven didn't know the truth about him.

And she would run away screaming if she did.

Better for both of them if he simply walked away. And he would, soon. But not as long as there was someone who planned to harm her.

Which meant he needed to find this guy, and soon. Satisfied with his plan, he filled two bowls with stew and carried them to the table, placing one in front of Raven. Then he cut two thick slices of bread and set those next to the bowls.

He took his usual seat across from her and bowed his head as Raven prayed over the food. It had been so long since he'd actually shared a meal with another person that he'd been shocked when she'd prayed at lunchtime.

Another reason to stay away. She was a believer, but he wasn't. If there was a God, why had He let Jack do the things he'd done? Why had He allowed Jack's men to suffer? And for Jack to be captured, held, and tortured in the Afghani prison?

These were questions without answers, and it took a minute for him to realize Raven had finished her prayer and was regarding him thoughtfully.

"God is watching over us, Jack."

He shrugged and picked up his spoon. He didn't want to fight or argue, considering how kind she'd been to him. "Maybe."

"I can hear your skepticism," she said with a smile. "And I understand it. I admit that after Daniel died, I spent a long time trying to figure out why God would allow something like that to happen. I mean, what did I do to deserve to become a widow at thirty?"

He looked at her curiously. "And what did you decide?"

"That God always has a plan. One that we might not understand. This past year and a half was hard, but I survived. And even grew stronger. Makes me wonder if you'd be sitting here now sharing venison stew with me if Daniel was still alive."

No way. The thought instantly popped into his mind. If he'd noticed a man around the cabin, he would have kept moving past without stopping.

The realization was jarring.

At the moment, he couldn't imagine not having met Raven. Having spent these few hours with her.

It was the first time in months that he'd felt civilized. Felt some semblance of normal.

Probably about as normal as he'd ever be. Which wasn't bad, since he hadn't attempted to hurt anyone since leaving Crystal Lake once and for all.

"I can see by your expression the answer is no. You wouldn't be here right now. And that means you wouldn't have noticed the footprints in the snow outside either." She waved her spoon at him. "It's not up to us to question God's plan. We can only ask for patience and guidance as we wait for His plan to be revealed."

Her words struck a chord deep within. Was Raven right about God's plan? He couldn't bring himself to believe it.

"The stew is delicious, but I ate too much of your food." He glanced at the slice of bread. "I've never made bread, but if you tell me what to do, I'll give it a try."

"Jack, I'd planned to make more bread in the morning." Her blue eyes danced with amusement. "As much as I'd love to watch you, frankly, it's easier for me to make it myself. And there's not that much standing involved."

"Okay." He still felt bad about eating so much of what she likely needed to survive on throughout winter. Unfortunately, he didn't have much cash. His last job had been well over a month ago. "I can hunt, if you'll let me borrow your shotgun."

She waved a hand at the fridge. "I still have plenty of venison."

"I could bring down a few turkeys for variety." As soon as the words left his mouth, he hastily added, "Although, it's not turkey or deer hunting season. Normally I trap animals to eat, but that might take too long."

"It's not that, I've been known to break that law in order to obtain food," Raven replied. "Turkey actually sounds good."

It was a testament to how far gone he was that he wanted to bring her a dozen turkeys. Crazy, because she didn't have room for that many. He was being ridiculous.

"I'll see what I can find." He finished the stew and then rose to take his bowl to the sink. "I'll wash the dishes again tonight."

"You're spoiling me," Raven protested. "You can do them tonight, but that's it. I'm sure my ankle will feel better by morning."

He hoped so, because staying much longer in the cabin with her was pure torture. It offered a hint as to what he'd never have.

What he didn't deserve.

But what about the intruder? He needed to figure out who that was and take care of the problem. Legally, he thought wryly.

When Raven finished her meal, he picked her up and carried her back to her sewing machine and quilt table. If her ankle was better in the morning, he'd miss carrying her around.

She was the only woman he'd touched in years.

He took the dogs outside again, letting them

romp around to burn off energy. The snow was still coming down, but lighter now, not an inch an hour. He figured it would stop sometime that night.

He watched Sadie closely, but the dog didn't growl at anything nearby. Was the intruder gone for good? Or would he come back later?

Doubtful the guy would return if he knew Jack was still there. If he'd seen Jack. Could be just the dog that had scared him away.

Still, Jack wasn't planning to take any chances. One thing the Army had taught him was how to set a trap. Not just for animals.

For people too.

For a moment he flashed to a Christmas four years ago, the last time he'd seen his brother from afar. When a woman and her son had been kidnapped by a man he presumed was her ex.

It gave him a small sense of satisfaction to know he'd helped save them both, the woman and her son. He'd set up trip wires and had disabled the kidnapper's car. He'd been prepared to do more, even if that meant sacrificing his freedom, but his brother had come to their rescue.

He was glad he'd been able to do something good for his brother, as a way of making up for the bad things he'd done.

And surprisingly, Ian had let him go. Over the years, Jack had dropped postcards along the way, letting Ian know that he was still alive. But always without a return address because he didn't want Ian coming to find him.

He longed to see his brother one more time, driven by a deep sense of urgency he didn't understand. Shaking off the flash of nostalgia, he called the dogs back and led them inside.

It was two hours before Raven had decided to call it a night. He'd carried her to the bathroom but wasn't quick enough to carry her from the bathroom to her bedroom. She'd called the dogs, and they happily joined her.

And maybe that was okay. The woman deserved some privacy. And he was beginning to like carrying her around, a little too much.

Jack stretched out on the sofa, watching the glowing embers through the glass of the wood-burning stove. He waited for a good hour, hoping Raven was a sound sleeper. Although waking the dogs was probably a higher risk. Sadie was an excellent watchdog.

When it was time to move, he pulled fishing line from his backpack. Tucking the knife in his pocket, just in case, he eased from the cabin and stood outside, listening to the silence.

Then he made his way around the perimeter of the cabin, stopping every so often to set up a series of trip wires.

If the intruder returned, Jack wanted to hear him coming. And stop him from getting too close.

When he finished setting the trip wires, he eased back into the cabin. He heard Belle whine a moment, but the dog quickly settled down.

He didn't sleep well on a good day and figured he wouldn't sleep at all enclosed in the cabin. Sure, it wasn't jail or the psych hospital, but walls around him had always brought on his claustrophobia.

But not this time. Raven's scent surrounded

him, and he closed his eyes and committed the moment to memory.

It was as close to happy as he'd been in a very long time.

~

RAVEN HADN'T EXPECTED to sleep well with a strange man in her home, but when Sadie and Belle woke her up to go outside, she was surprised to see that dawn was peeking up just over the horizon.

Sitting up abruptly, it hit her that the snow had stopped. In fact, the brightness of the snow made everything look crisp and fresh and new.

On the heels of that thought was the knowledge that Jack would leave today.

She told herself that was what she'd wanted, just to offer him respite from the storm. But that wasn't entirely true any longer.

Spending the day with him had been really nice. And not just because he'd done all the chores.

But because she'd enjoyed spending time with him.

She looked at her ankle, relieved to see that it was less swollen. Maybe sitting around all day, and having Jack carry her around, had provided enough rest for the injury to heal.

Using the cane, she made her way out of the bedroom. The dogs ran ahead, eager to go outside. She stopped when she saw Jack standing there, looking sleepily rumpled.

"My ankle is much better," she blurted before

he tried to carry her again. "Will you do me a favor and let the dogs out?"

"Sure." He turned away. "Come, Sadie, Belle."

While he took care of the dogs, she quickly used the bathroom, changed, and hobbled to the kitchen. She wished she could offer Jack more than oatmeal, but she didn't have any eggs. A repeat of yesterday's coffee and oatmeal would have to do.

She watched through the window as Jack played with the dogs, especially Belle who seemed both agitated and excited with the snow. She was touched when she noticed he'd used his boot to clear a spot to make it easier for Belle to do her doggie business.

She may not know much about Jack Keller, but he was kind and gentle. More so even than Daniel had been.

No, it wasn't fair to compare the two men. Daniel was gone, and he had been a good husband.

Jack was a drifter passing through.

"Something smells great," Jack said when he entered the cabin with the dogs a few minutes later.

"Just oatmeal and coffee." She glanced at him over her shoulder. "Sleep okay?"

"Yes. You?" Jack took a moment to stuff wood into the stove, before joining her in the kitchen.

"Great." Why did the conversation suddenly seem so stilted? She poured a large mug of coffee and slid it over to him. "I'm glad the storm has stopped."

He nodded, taking a sip of the coffee. She

spooned oatmeal into bowls and handed him one before taking a seat. Then she bowed her head and softly prayed, loud enough for Jack to hear her. "Dear Lord, we thank You for this food we are about to eat. We also ask that you keep us safe from harm and continue to guide us on Your chosen path. Amen."

There was a pause before Jack echoed, "Amen."

She jerked her head up in surprise. "I thought you didn't believe?"

He shrugged and picked up his spoon. "You've been very kind to me, Raven. I wanted to be polite."

So he didn't really believe but pretended to? Or maybe he didn't want to let himself believe? Since he'd be heading out shortly, she let it go.

Jack would need to find his own path to God. She couldn't do that for him.

"Raven, I would like to ask a favor of you."

His serious tone sent a warning chill down her spine. "What is that?"

"I'd like you to drive into Crystal Lake and report the strange footprints in the snow to the sheriff's department." His green gaze pierced her. "It's important for you to have a paper trail in case he tries anything else."

She considered his request as she finished her oatmeal. "Will you come with me?"

He hesitated, then said, "I wouldn't mind getting a ride into town."

"All right, I'll file a report." She knew it was the right thing to do, but she also felt like it was a bit of an overreaction. "I'm not sure the police will take it seriously though."

He didn't respond but finished his meal and then carried their dirty dishes to the sink. "If you don't mind, I'd like to use your shower again."

"Of course, help yourself."

"Thanks." He drank more coffee and washed the dishes, before disappearing into the bathroom. She battled a wave of sorrow at his leaving.

Crazy to realize how much she'd miss him.

When it was time to go, she hid a wince as she pulled her boots on over her injured ankle. But surprisingly the added support helped more than wrapping it in Christmas fabric had.

"Should we bring the dogs?" Jack asked, waiting by the door.

"Why not?" She pulled on her dark blue parka. "Come, Belle. Come, Sadie."

Jack held the door open, but then went ahead to forge a path to the garage. She let the dogs in the back, then slid into the driver's seat.

"I assume this truck has four-wheel drive," he said.

"Of course." She scoffed as she drove out of the garage, bulldozing her way through the snow. "I have a four-wheeler with a plow on the front too."

He frowned. "If I'd have known, I'd have carved a path for you."

"I don't bother when I'm not planning to go anywhere." She cranked the wheel and eased on the gas, rumbling down the paved driveway. "Where would you like to be dropped off?"

"Let's get to the sheriff's department headquarters first." Jack looked curiously out the window. "Not many people out today."

"The plows haven't been through yet. And there aren't many tourists here this time of year. Except for some snowmobilers."

"I stay far away from those," he said absently.

She didn't blame him. The noise of the engines was terrible and not at all what living in the woods meant.

Her truck moved fairly well through the snow-covered roads, and when she turned onto Main Street, Jack looked around with blatant curiosity.

"It hasn't changed much," he said, seemingly talking to himself.

"Not this time of the year," she acknowledged. "But in the summer it's really busy with tourists. Which is good for me as I depend on those tourists spending money on quilts."

Jack's expression closed up as she turned into the plowed parking lot of the sheriff's department headquarters. She put the gearshift into park and turned to face him. "Nervous about going inside?"

He turned to look at her. "I'm sorry, but I can't come inside with you, Raven." His voice was so quiet she had trouble hearing him.

"Why not?"

"I want you to ask for Deputy Ian Kramer," he said, ignoring her question. "And if for some reason Ian Kramer isn't working today, then ask for Devon Armbruster." He paused, then added, "The only other name I know is Sheriff Torretti, but I don't think he's the best one to take a report."

"If these deputies know your brother, then you

should come in and say hi. After all, you're planning to visit, aren't you?"

There was a long silence before he said, "Ian Kramer is my brother. But I can't come in with you because there's likely an outstanding warrant out for my arrest. So please, just go in and ask for Ian Kramer or Devon Armbruster, okay?"

"Arrest? For what?"

His eyes darkened with regret and shame as he shook his head. "Better you don't know."

There was so much she wanted to ask but knew it would be futile. His closed expression didn't invite further comments. She'd sensed there was more to Jack's story than he let on, but this? An active warrant for his arrest?

She pushed open her door and eased down from the vehicle, her thoughts whirling. It was obvious that his forcing her to come into town in order to file a complaint had been a huge risk for Jack.

She took some solace in knowing that he cared more about her safety than his.

6

____

Shame burned deep in his soul as he watched Raven hobble into the sheriff's department headquarters using his cane for support. He knew he'd scared her with the information about having an open arrest warrant, and even worse was the fact that she didn't know any of the gory details. If she did, she'd regret ever letting him inside her cabin.

And if he was as good a man as he'd been trying to be, he would have left regardless of her insisting he stay.

The truth hurt, but he shoved the flash of regret away. He'd carried the guilt of what he'd done for a long time. Those first few months he'd been home after Afghanistan had been a blur. But he knew he'd threatened to hurt people. To kill them.

And he'd started a fire, hurting the very thing he loved the most.

The wilderness.

He squeezed his eyes shut against the memory. If he could take back what he'd done, he would. But there was no erasing his past mistakes.

Being in the psychiatric hospital had been awful, reminding him of being held prisoner in Afghanistan. Except maybe for the torture he'd experienced at his captor's hands. The scars had faded over time, those on his skin and those in his mind.

When he'd seen a chance to escape, he'd acted swiftly and never looked back. In fact, he'd left every trace of his former self behind, starting fresh with a new name and identity. He'd succeeded in his goal, had stayed far away from civilization so that he wouldn't harm anyone else.

Something he'd managed to accomplish, until now.

He'd allowed himself to get close to Raven.

Too close.

Better to stay far away from everyone else to avoid the possibility of a relapse.

It was time to move on. The only thing that bothered him was that the intruder was still out there, somewhere. He didn't buy the theory that he was lost and looking for a ride, scared away when he caught a glimpse of Jack. In fact, the opposite. He felt certain anyone looking for a ride would have been happy to see a couple inside.

Only a man who wanted to catch Raven alone would sneak away.

Maybe he'd camp in the woods behind Raven's property for a while, to see if anyone returned. He stared down at his hands for a moment. He'd just have to make sure that he simply held anyone he caught until the police arrived.

He blew out a deep breath, decision made. Raven wouldn't want to share her cabin with a criminal. Besides, she deserved to have her home to herself. And the dogs.

Jack decided to wait until she returned before leaving. He wanted to hear what his brother may have told her. Granted, walking back to her cabin would take time, but he felt certain the intruder, coward that he was, would wait until dark to return.

Belle whined and tried to lick him. His heart squeezed as he gently stroked the puppy. The sweet ball of fur that had wiggled through his rough exterior and into his heart.

Raven was inside the building for longer than he'd expected, and he hoped that was a good sign that they were taking her situation seriously.

When she emerged a few minutes later, he slid out of the passenger seat. "Did you talk to Ian? How did it go?"

Raven shrugged. "Devon Armbruster took my statement, but he just told me to call if I see anything more. Sounds like there isn't much they can do about it."

He nodded in agreement. It was what he'd expected. "Ian must be off today."

Raven surprised him by putting a hand on his arm. "Jack, I was told that Ian Kramer was out on medical leave until after the first of the year."

He went stock-still, the news swimming in his brain. "Medical leave? For what?"

He was grateful for the connection of her hand on his arm. "They wouldn't tell me because of the privacy laws. But based on the serious expression in Devon Armbruster's eyes, I think you might want to head over to see him as soon as possible."

"Yes, thanks." Was this the strange sense of urgency he'd felt to see Ian again? He needed to go but found himself staring at Raven, trying to think of a way to say goodbye and to thank her for what she'd done for him.

He turned away, but Raven tightened her grip on his arm. "Wait."

"It's time for me to go."

Her wide blue eyes clung to his, and then she completely surprised him by coming up close and kissing him.

Her lips were warm and sweet, and the spark of desire short-circuited the wires in his brain. He knew there was something he needed to do, but he couldn't remember. Instead, he wrapped his arms around her and kissed her back, the way he hadn't kissed anyone since before he'd been deployed overseas.

Finally, he forced himself to lift his head. Maybe Raven had kissed him, but she still didn't know everything he'd done. He dragged in a deep breath and forced his thoughts into some kind of order. "I have to go," he repeated, feeling dazed.

"Will you come back to the cabin after seeing your brother?" She held on to his shoulders as if she couldn't stand on her own two feet.

He wanted more than anything to say yes, but he knew that would be wrong. He glanced around for her cane, finding it on the ground where she'd dropped it. He gently set her aside to retrieve it.

"I don't think that's a good idea." He handed her the cane.

Her fingers tightened on his jacket as if she wanted to shake him, but she reluctantly let him go. She took the cane and turned toward her truck.

He opened the back door, shooed the dogs back from the door, and reached for his backpack. He gave Belle one last caress before shutting the door.

"I don't care what you've done in the past, Jack." Raven's voice was clear and strong. "I know you're a good, kind, and caring man."

Her words made his throat swell with regret intermingled with hope. Emotions he hadn't felt for a long time.

It was easy for her to say those words when she didn't know the extent of his crimes.

And he couldn't bear to tell her.

Jack slung the backpack over his shoulder. "Goodbye, Raven. Thanks for everything."

Without waiting for a response, he turned and walked away.

HER LIPS TINGLING from the impact of Jack's kiss, Raven helplessly watched him walk away, wishing she could think of a way to convince him to stay.

She slid behind the wheel, stashing the cane in the passenger seat. It had been tempting to ask Deputy Armbruster about Jack Keller's background, but she was afraid he'd instantly come outside to arrest him.

She gripped the steering wheel tightly, reliving their kiss. It had been a year and a half since she'd kissed a man. And she was rather shocked at herself for instigating it. But the thought of never seeing Jack again made her desperate.

If a kiss was all she'd have to remember him by, she'd take it.

She started the truck and headed down the street, pulling up alongside Jack. He glanced at her, then hunched his shoulders and kept walking.

Lowering the passenger side window, she shouted, "Jack, I'll give you a ride to your brother's place."

He drew in a deep breath, then stopped and ducked his head to answer through the open window. "I'll be fine, Raven."

"But why not take the ride?" She persisted. "I can get you there soon, and I know you're concerned about him."

A flash of uncertainty flickered over his features. "You should get home; you have a quilt to make."

Why was he being so stubborn? "Jack, please. Let me do this for you. I'd be worried about my sibling being on medical leave that I didn't know anything about." When he didn't move, she lost her temper. "Get in the truck!"

The corner of his mouth tipped up in a crooked smile, which made her shake her head, wondering why he thought her flash of temper was so funny.

"Okay." He opened the back passenger door and was greeted with sloppy kisses from Belle as he placed his backpack in the well behind the seat. He scratched Belle behind the ears before closing the door and climbing in beside her.

She raised the window and put the truck in gear. "Are you always this difficult?"

He glanced at her with amusement. "Me? How about you?"

"It's not a big deal for me to offer you a ride." She shook her head wondering why she was bothering to explain. "I need directions."

Jack peered through the window. "Ian lives in a house tucked in the woods, similar to yours, but not as far out of town if I remember correctly." When she headed out on the highway in the opposite direction from where her place was located, he gestured with his hand. "I think it's about a mile down from here, on the right."

She drove slowly, keeping a keen eye out for anything resembling a driveway. After a mile, she slowed to a stop. "Did I miss it?"

Jack frowned. "It could be two miles out, try going a little farther."

She'd only driven another fifty feet when she saw what appeared to be a driveway. "Is that it?"

"Yeah." Jack looked tense as she carefully took the corner into the driveway.

It hadn't been plowed, which made her wonder what ailment was keeping Ian Kramer down. She sent up a prayer that it was nothing too serious.

Jack looked as if he might be holding his breath, every muscle in his body growing more tense as she approached the house. When the dwelling came into view, there was smoke coming from the chimney indicating someone was home.

"You can let me off here," Jack said in a hoarse tone. "I don't know that he's up for visitors."

She understood what he meant. It was one thing for a brother to stop by, it was something different to have a total stranger on your doorstep. Bringing the truck to a halt, she watched as he jumped down and retrieved his pack.

"Thanks for the ride." His green gaze was dark with fear and worry. Leaving Jack there and turning the truck around to drive away was the hardest thing she'd ever done.

But this homecoming wasn't about her. She told herself to be glad Jack was returning to his family after being gone for so long.

She watched Jack through her rearview mirror until she couldn't see him any longer.

And instantly felt a suffocating crush of loneliness as she turned toward home.

Jack eased into the trees surrounding his brother's house, planning to watch the place before barging in.

What if Ian had sold the property to someone else? He didn't want to frighten the new owners.

Although, deep down, he didn't think so. Ian used a PO Box for his mail and could be anywhere, but Jack felt certain his brother would have remained in the same spot.

Maybe hoping one day Jack would return.

He stayed in the trees for at least fifteen minutes, just watching and waiting. For what, he wasn't sure. Was he expecting Ian to come out and find him? It was odd that no one inside noticed the truck pull into the driveway and then turn around and leave again.

Unless that sort of thing happened often.

No, more likely they were busy. Maybe he should come back later.

Coward, his mind taunted.

Right. He was being ridiculous. He forced himself to walk up to the front door of the house where he and Ian had grown up. Ian, or whoever lived here now, had kept the place in good shape. Whatever Ian was struggling with must not have been going on too long, the trim had been freshly painted in the past few months.

He lifted his hand and knocked sharply on the door. There were thumps from inside, then the sound of footsteps approaching. He held his breath, waiting for what seemed like an eternity for the door to open.

When it did, a dark-haired woman stood there, holding a toddler on her hip. Her gaze was pleasant but wary. "Yes?"

"Ah, I don't know if I have the right house, is Ian Kramer here?"

She stared at him intently, the little girl on her hip sucking her thumb and playing with her pigtail. It took Ian a moment to realize this was the same woman whom he'd watched being dragged with her son through the woods almost exactly four years ago. "May I ask what this is about?"

"I'm, uh, his brother. J-Jesse." It had been a long time since he'd spoken his real name out loud.

Her eyes widened in shocked surprise, and he realized she was struck by fear.

"I'm not here to hurt anyone," he hastily reassured her. "I just wanted to see Ian. If he's here."

"You're Jesse!" The dark-haired woman smiled so broadly he was taken aback by her reaction. "Oh, I've prayed and prayed for this day! Come in, please." She stepped back from the door, calling over her shoulder, "Ian? God has answered our prayers! Jesse's here."

God had answered their prayers? He wondered if he'd somehow stepped into an alternate universe. Why would anyone be glad to see a wanted criminal show up on their doorstep?

Especially a woman with a child?

"Come in," she said again. "Please."

He forced himself to cross the threshold, glancing around with interest. A boy, the one he remembered from four years ago, yet obviously older now, stood tall next to his father.

Ian. Jake's throat tightened when he got a glimpse of his brother. At first he thought Ian looked similar to the way he had before, but then he noticed his brother was pale and moved slower than normal.

"Jesse! I can't believe you're really here!" As if there were no hard feelings between them, Ian came over and gave him a big hug.

Was it his imagination or was Ian weaker than he had been?

"It's good to see you too," he managed, patting Ian on the back. "It's been a long time."

"Too long," Ian said, taking a step back. He eyed Jack curiously. "You look good, Jesse."

He was suddenly glad he'd cleaned up at Raven's house. The old version of him would have scared the woman and children, no question. "Thanks. I, uh, you should know I'm going by the name of Jack now. Jack Keller. I, um, have a Michigan ID in that name."

Ian's brow furrowed, and Jack wondered if he'd said too much. His brother was still a cop, after all. "I can understand that. Please, sit down. Can we get you something to drink? Oh, and this is my wife, Sarah, our son Ben, and our daughter Grace. Ethan is here somewhere too. Oh, there he is."

A kid who looked to be about five came running out with a dump truck in his hand. "Vroom, vroom!"

"It's nice to meet you in person, Jesse. Or, Jack." Sarah flushed and bent to set Grace down. "Go and play now," she told the little ones. "Ben, would you please take them into the playroom?"

"I guess." Ben didn't look thrilled with the task but did as he was told.

"You have a wonderful family, Ian." He sat on the edge of an overstuffed chair feeling nervous. "I'm glad."

"Thanks. I couldn't be happier." Ian reached up to draw Sarah close. "We've been very blessed."

Jack could see how happy they were and ignored the tiny flash of envy. He cleared his throat. "I won't stay long, I just wanted to check in." He paused, then added, "I heard you were out on medical leave."

Ian's brow shot up. "Where did you hear that?"

All this talking was exhausting after being alone for so long, but he quickly filled his brother in on the footprints outside the snow of Raven Clark's cabin and his insistence she notify the police.

"I haven't met Raven, but I have one of her quilts. She does incredible work," Sarah said with a smile.

It was nice to hear, but he kept his gaze trained on Ian. "Are you okay?"

Ian nodded. "I am now, yes. I was in the hospital though, ended up with leukemia."

"Leukemia?" Jack couldn't have been more surprised.

"Yes, that's one of the reasons we've been praying for you, Jesse." Sarah's gaze was gentle. "For a while we thought Ian wasn't going to make it, and all we wanted was for him to see you again. Thankfully, Ian got better and now you're here. God has answered all of our prayers in the best way possible."

Jack stared at his brother and his wife, stunned by the realization that God may have provided the sense of urgency for him to return.

Humbling to know that if he'd ignored God's plan, he might have missed his last chance to see his brother.

7

Raven had gotten all the way back to her cabin, letting the dogs run loose, when she decided to turn around and head back into town. This time, she put the dogs inside before heading out. Maybe it was crazy, but her curiosity about Jack wouldn't let her alone, and Josie, the owner of Rose's Café, was the biggest gossip she knew.

Normally, she avoided gossip, not really interested in who was doing what with whom. But if anyone knew the history behind an outstanding warrant for Jack's arrest, it was Josie.

She parked in front of the diner, then hesitated, second-guessing her decision. Would it raise suspicions if she pried into Jack's case? Carla mentioned Josie knew everything about everyone, and if she thought Jack was back in town, the owner of the diner might just decide to call the police.

There was also the fact that she didn't normally spend her hard-earned cash in the diner. And the secret of Jack's past was his to tell.

Except he hadn't. Instead, he'd walked away.

Muttering to herself, she pushed open the driver's side door and used Jack's cane to make her way inside. It was between the breakfast and lunch hour, so she was able to find a seat at the counter easily enough.

"Hello, Raven, isn't it?" Josie beamed at her. "Did you bring more quilts to Carla? I believe she sold your last one yesterday."

"Really?" She was pleased to hear the news and made a mental note to stop by Carla's Crafts after she was finished. "That's great."

"What can I get you?" Josie held her notepad at the ready.

"Is it too late for breakfast? I'd love two eggs over easy with hash browns and bacon." Bacon and eggs were a luxury, but she deserved a reward for selling all of her Christmas quilts.

Next year, she'd have to make more.

"Of course not! Coming right up." Josie filled a cup of coffee and set it in front of her.

"Oh, I'm sorry, I didn't necessarily want coffee," she protested.

"It's on the house," Josie said. Then frowned. "Unless you don't like coffee?"

She blushed and cradled the mug in her hands, relishing the warmth. "I love coffee. Just had my quota for the day, that's all."

"Quota schmota," Josie said with a laugh. "I couldn't run this place without coffee, it keeps me going."

Josie's coffee was great, and she let herself enjoy it as Josie put in her order, then returned to the counter. "What's new with you?"

"Me? Nothing really." Raven stared down at her mug, then drummed up the courage to say, "I just heard about Ian Kramer being out on medical leave. I hope he's okay."

Josie nodded sagely. "Sarah told me he was pretty sick at first, but he's home and doing much better now." She tilted her head curiously. "I didn't realize you knew Ian and Sarah Kramer."

"Oh, I don't know them personally, but I heard the news when I stopped at the sheriff's department." Her face was growing so red, she felt certain Josie knew she was prying. "I'm glad to hear he's okay. I'll keep him and his family in my prayers."

"Good idea," Josie said with a nod. "Have you been attending church services?"

"More so in the summer than the winter." Once Sadie had given birth to her litter of pups, leaving for even a couple of hours had been impossible. When she did attend services, she sat in the back and never lingered to chat with Pastor John afterward.

Which was pretty antisocial now that she thought about it.

"I'll do better from now on," she said out loud.

"Oh, honey, I'm not judging you," Josie assured her. "We can pray anywhere, can't we? God listens no matter what."

That made her smile. "Yes, absolutely."

The mention of God made her ashamed of the reason she'd come here, prying for information on Jack's past. Hadn't she told him she didn't care what he'd done?

It was none of her business.

Josie moved away to serve another customer. When Raven's breakfast came, she relished the eggs, bacon, and potatoes. She left Josie a nice tip and then slid off her stool, leaning on her cane.

"You okay, Raven?" Josie asked with concern.

"Fine, really. Just tripped over my puppy, that's all." Raven smiled. "Thanks for breakfast, Josie."

"Anytime, Raven. Don't be a stranger now, ya hear?"

"I won't." Raven walked outside and headed down the street to Carla's craft store. As long as she was here, she may as well pick up her earnings and do a little shopping.

Maybe she'd splurge on a couple of cartons of eggs.

As she approached the craft shop, she noticed a man walking toward her. A sneer was etched on his features, and she was taken aback by the venom in his gaze.

He was the right age to be Sean Calloway, but she didn't like thinking the worst about people. Doing her best to ignore him, she quickly darted inside the shop.

"Hi, Raven," Carla greeted her cheerfully. "Did you bring more quilts?"

"I wish," Raven said with a smile. "I heard from Josie that you sold all my Christmas quilts. What a blessing!"

"I did, and I have a waiting list for two more, if you have time to make them." Carla gestured for her to come inside. "I still have one of your wedding quilts from last year but managed to sell everything else. Your work is amazing."

Raven blushed. "Thanks, and I'm happy to

make two more quilts, but I don't think I'll be able to finish them before Christmas."

"They don't care," Carla assured her. "They'll take them when you have them finished."

"Okay, then, I'll start working on them as soon as I get home." She glanced over her shoulder, checking to see if the scowling man was outside. "Carla, since I don't have any more quilts for you, maybe you could show some of Sean Calloway's work for a few weeks?"

Carla's expression softened. "That's sweet of you, Raven, but he's so upset I doubt he'd bring anything in, especially on a short-term basis."

"I—think I saw him outside just now. If looks could kill . . ." Her voice trailed off, and she wondered if Jack had been right about the intruder peering into her cabin. After seeing the frank hatred in Sean's eyes, she could easily imagine him doing such a thing.

"Yeah, he spends a lot of time up at the pub." Carla shrugged. "I have to do what's best for my business."

"Absolutely," Raven agreed. She smiled. "I guess I'll keep Sean in my prayers too."

Carla rummaged in her cash drawer and drew out a thick envelope. "Here's what you've earned so far, and more to come once you finish up those last two Christmas quilts."

"Thanks, Carla." Raven gratefully took the cash and buttoned it in the pocket of her coat. "I'm glad people seem to like them."

"Me too," Carla agreed. "Happy sewing!"

Raven left the shop and returned to her truck, noting with relief the scowling man was gone.

After a quick stop at the grocery store, she returned to her cabin, this time intending to stay.

The cabin seemed ridiculously quiet and empty, even though the dogs greeted her with enthusiasm. Having had a second mid-morning breakfast, she decided to work through lunch.

But as she measured and began cutting triangles and squares for a new Christmas quilt, she couldn't help wondering about Jack.

Was he still visiting his brother? Or had he already headed out to his next destination? If he'd left, he was no doubt already far, far away.

Dear Lord, please continue to guide Jack on Your chosen path. Amen.

~

JACK HADN'T PLANNED to stay for lunch, but Sarah and Ian insisted. Surprisingly, being inside the house where he and Ian had grown up didn't cause his claustrophobia to return.

Or maybe he was finally putting those torturous months in Afghan captivity behind him for good.

"Are there chores you'd like me to do before I leave? Need more wood chopped?" Jack asked when they'd finished with the homemade chicken noodle soup Sarah had served.

"I'm not an invalid, Jesse. I mean, Jack." Ian was having trouble remembering his new name. Which was understandable since he'd been Jesse his whole life. "The doc said I can resume normal activities, and while I might have to stop more frequently for rest breaks, I'm able to chop my own wood."

"I'm sure you can," Jack agreed. "But I'm here to help."

"Will you stay through Christmas?" Sarah asked, bringing in a tray of chocolate chip cookies for dessert. "We'd love to have you."

"Ah, I don't know." His gaze landed on a large wall calendar that Sarah used to keep track of the kids' activities. "I don't want to impose for five whole days."

"You're not imposing," Ian argued. "We'd love to have you."

He leveled a serious gaze at his brother. "Do you think that's a good idea, Ian? You're a sheriff's deputy, and I'm sure there is still a warrant out for my arrest."

Ian waved that off. "First of all, I'm not entirely convinced there is an open warrant out there. But if there is, I know for a fact no one is actively looking for you."

Jack didn't believe him. "I'm sorry, Ian, but I'm not going back. I've been doing well on my own by staying away from civilization."

"I'm glad to hear that, J-ack." Ian glanced at Sarah. "I wanted to thank you for what you did for Sarah and Ben four years ago. We wouldn't have found them so quickly without your help."

"I wasn't far away," Jack confessed. "In fact, I was about to come out of hiding when you showed up."

Sarah surprised him by enveloping him in a quick hug. "Thank you," she whispered.

All this attention was unnerving. Why weren't

they talking about the bad things he'd done? The people he'd nearly killed? The fire he'd set?

"I have to go," he abruptly stood, needing space. But then his gaze landed on Ian. "Are you sure you're better? Or do you have additional doctor's appointments coming up?"

"I always have doctor's appointments," Ian muttered with disgust. "But the good news is that my last blood work was great. No need to worry about a bone marrow transplant."

That news caught him off guard. "A bone marrow transplant? Don't you need a match for that?"

"Yes, we do," Sarah said softly. "Unfortunately, I wasn't a match and neither were any of the kids. There was a good chance of finding a donor through the tissue bank though. Thankfully, we didn't need to go that route."

"What about me? Couldn't I be a match?" He stared at his brother. "Is that why you were praying for me to come home?"

"Je-Jack, I prayed because I wanted to see you before I died." Ian's gaze never left his. "And as it turned out, I don't need a bone marrow transplant."

But he almost had. Jack felt sick at the thought of his brother lying in a hospital bed, waiting for some anonymous donor because his brother was hiding in the forest.

No wonder God sent him back here, with urgency. "Listen, Ian, I won't leave until I give a tissue sample, in case you need it sometime in the future."

Sarah and Ian exchanged a look. "That's fine,

Jack, but really, it's not necessary. I'm fine, should be able to return to work after the first of the year."

There was a long minute of silence before Sarah said, "I meant what I said about sharing Christmas with you." She kept her voice low, likely so the kids wouldn't hear. "Please, think about it, okay? Even if you can't stay now, maybe you'll find your way back in time for the holiday."

It was on the tip of his tongue to refuse again, but then he remembered his plan to camp outside Raven's cabin. Even if he managed to get the guy who'd been sneaking around her property, why not stay a couple more days?

Especially since he planned to make good on his promise to be tested as a potential bone marrow donor. He wasn't sure what that entailed, but he didn't think he could just walk in from the street to have that done. He'd need an appointment at the very least.

"I will," he said slowly. "Be back for Christmas, I mean."

"Really?" Sarah's face brightened as if she'd been given a million bucks. "That's wonderful! Thank you so much!"

She hugged him again, as did Ian. As he walked out with his backpack over his shoulder, it occurred to him that he'd been hugged by more people in the past two days than he had in four years.

Surprisingly, he didn't mind it, considering he'd avoided any and all human contact since returning stateside.

Thoughts of Raven's kiss kept him warm as he

hiked back through the woods in the general direction of her cabin. The deep snow made it slow going, and he had to squelch the temptation to head back to Ian's and ask for a ride.

Telling himself not to be lazy, he purposefully picked up the pace, pushing himself to cover more ground at a faster clip. He'd avoided the road, mostly because he didn't want to be seen, but walking cross country took more strength and endurance. It was a good thing he had a map of the area imprinted on his brain, or he may not be able to find his way back to Raven.

Not Raven, he mentally corrected. To her cabin. And only to make sure the intruder didn't show up again.

As the sun dipped on the horizon, he walked faster, hoping to reach her place before dark.

When he saw the familiar smoke rising from Raven's cabin, he felt an overwhelming sense of relief. There was at least a half hour of daylight left.

Slowing his pace, he searched the trees for signs of roosting turkeys. It had occurred to him that he could repay Raven for everything she'd done by trapping one. After all, she'd mentioned how nice it would be to have a change from venison.

When he had her cabin within view, he made a wide berth so that he was on the opposite side of the cabin a few yards from where he'd set his trip wires. He found a good place between two trees to make camp.

It didn't take him long. When that was finished, he quickly put together a sling foot turkey trap and walked through the woods for a good place to set it up.

He baited the trap with birdseed that he carried specifically for this purpose, then melted into the brush to wait.

The snow may have worked in his favor because it didn't take long for a hen to drop into his trap. With her foot tangled in the rope, he easily grabbed her.

Living off the land was often brutal, and he always felt bad for killing wild creatures. Yet his survival instincts were strong, and food was necessary to stay alive.

The light faded away as he began the work of field dressing the turkey. When he finished, he took the bird up to Raven's front door. He knocked, then moved back.

"Jack! What are you doing here?" She looked genuinely surprised and happy to see him.

"I wanted to leave you dinner." He gestured at the bird. "It's my way of saying thanks."

"A turkey!" Her enthusiasm made him smile. Only a woman like Raven would be excited by such a gift. "Why don't you come inside and share it with me?"

He took another step back because he was all too tempted to join her. "No, it's for you, Raven."

Was it his imagination or was she disappointed? He reminded himself that she knew nothing of the details surrounding his arrest.

"How was your meeting with Ian?"

He nodded slowly. "Good. He was sick with leukemia, but he is better now."

Her mouth formed a small O. "Wow, it's a good thing God sent you here."

"Yes, it is." He was starting to believe that God had indeed guided him here. "Goodbye, Raven."

"Goodbye." Her voice had a plaintive note that was nearly impossible to ignore.

But he managed, by some sort of herculean effort.

Back in his tent, he listened carefully for any sound indicating the intruder might have returned.

Silently longing for something he'd never have.

8

R aven had placed the wild turkey Jack had trapped and dressed into a deep roasting pan, wishing for the tenth time that she hadn't let him walk away.

Not that she was strong enough to physically hold him against his will. The idea of attempting such a thing was ludicrous.

The scent of the roasting turkey was enough to make her mouth water, yet it felt wrong to eat the wonderful meal without Jack. After all, he'd done the work of trapping the bird. She'd finished cutting the fabric and begun designing the pattern, determined to get a nice start on the two additional Christmas quilts Carla had requested. It was humbling to know her quilts were doing so well, and she sent up a silent prayer of gratitude to God for watching over her.

As always, her thoughts strayed back to Jack like a homing pigeon. Hopefully, he'd find a way back to his faith. No easy task for someone who had gone through what he had. He hadn't said much about his time in Afghanistan, but the wounded expression in his eyes indicated he'd endured something terrible.

And had paid the ultimate price. Losing a small piece of his heart and soul. And only God could heal his wounds.

She finished her design and pulled the roasting pan from the oven. She carved the bird, putting a good portion of the meat away in the freezer for future meals, and the bones in the fridge to make soup.

Eating alone hadn't bothered her for the past year, but as she bowed her head to pray, she found herself wishing once again that Jack was with her. She didn't understand how she'd grown so dependent on him in such a short time.

No, dependent wasn't the right word. More like accustomed to. She could handle things herself, the way she always had, but she missed his company.

His presence.

His kiss.

Enough. This foolishness had to stop. Time to get over him already. Two days did not make a relationship. She'd been with Daniel for months before they'd gotten married.

She bit into her meal and smiled with appreciation. The turkey was a wonderful change from venison, and she had Jack to thank for it.

Her ankle was throbbing after all the weight she'd put on it that day, so she continued using Jack's cane to take care of the dogs.

Outside, the snow glistened with moonlight. She walked around the front of the cabin, searching for signs of Jack's tent, but of course, she didn't see anything.

If not for his dropping the turkey on her doorstep, she would have assumed he'd stayed with Ian.

Belle let out several barks, struggling to get through the deep snow. "Come, Belle. Come!"

The puppy hesitated, then turned and ran back to her side. Sadie sniffed the air intently, likely scenting a wild animal. Last spring, Sadie had found a skunk family and Raven had feared she'd never get rid of that awful smell.

Thankfully, skunks didn't come out in winter.

"Come, Sadie." The dogs followed her inside, and she was relieved they hadn't scented anything unusual. If there had been a strange man lurking nearby, Sadie would have let her know.

Sean Calloway? Or Taylor Wilkes? She didn't really think Brian Flynn, the creepy mechanic from the garage, was involved.

But that night she couldn't sleep, her brain darting off in different directions.

The isolation of the cabin located far from civilization had gone from being a comfort to depressing loneliness.

And deep down, she felt certain the change had come from enjoying the brief time she'd had with Jack.

The next morning, she hobbled into the kitchen to make coffee. Lots and lots of coffee to make up for her restless night.

There was no way to blame her lack of sleep on the intruder, since he'd never returned.

As she pulled a few precious eggs from her

fridge to splurge on for breakfast, a familiar sound reached her ears.

What in the world?

Sadie and Belle were both whining at the door. Seeing Jack chopping a log into sections had her shaking her head in bemusement.

It didn't make any sense. If he'd camped nearby, why not share dinner with her?

Unless her bold kiss had scared him off.

She filled a mug with coffee, then drew on her coat and pulled on her boots to head outside. The dogs made a beeline for Jack, Belle jumping all over him with unabashed excitement.

"Hey, Belle." He removed his gloves and crouched down to pet the puppy. She wiggled close, licking his chin. Sadie came over too, her tail wagging but at least showing some restraint.

"I thought you'd be long gone by now." She held out the coffee.

Jack hesitated, then accepted the mug. "I felt the need to keep an eye on the place."

His words felt like a bucket of ice water being thrown in her face. He hadn't stayed for her, specifically, but because of the intruder.

The fact that he'd refused to join her for dinner had to be related to his desire to stay away from her on a personal level.

She should have never kissed him. Although to be fair, she'd thought that was the last time she'd see him.

"I'm sorry," she offered lamely.

He sipped more coffee, eyeing her over the rim. "For what?"

She glanced away, feeling embarrassed he was making her explain. "I shouldn't have kissed you."

He sputtered and coughed, his eyes starting to water.

"Are you okay? Or do you need the Heimlich maneuver?"

"I'm fine," he managed between coughing fits. "Swallowed wrong."

She eyed the fallen log. "Where did you find that?"

"In the woods." After a minute, he handed her the empty mug and picked up the ax. "Thanks for the coffee. I'll finish this up for you."

Was he really going to ignore her apology without saying anything in response? What did that mean?

"I'm having eggs for breakfast. Would you like some? I have plenty to share."

He hoisted the ax over his shoulder and brought it down with a jarring thud. Then he turned to look at her. "Raven, I'm trying to pay you back for everything you've done for me, but you keep offering to do more. At this rate, I'll never repay my debt."

She felt sad for him. "This isn't about paying back a debt, Jack. I invited you to share a meal with me, no ulterior motive involved. Life isn't all checks and balances. There is always the option of simply paying it forward. Do something nice for someone else down the road."

He stared at her for so long she thought maybe he'd zoned out again, the way he had at one point yesterday. But then he sighed. "You have a point. I would enjoy sharing breakfast with you,

Raven. Just let me finish this section of wood, okay?"

"Okay." Light-headed with relief, she turned and headed back inside. "Come, Sadie, Belle."

The dogs happily joined her, as if sensing Jack would be in soon.

And even though she knew Jack's presence here was only temporary, she used the time to freshen up as if this was some sort of date.

Crazy, because she hadn't been on a date in years.

Still, she was female enough to want Jack to see her looking her best. Even though he would be leaving soon.

Taking a tiny piece of her heart with him.

~

JACK CALLED himself all kinds of a fool for agreeing to have breakfast with Raven. Why was he finding it so difficult to stay away from her?

One surefire way to get rid of these invitations would be to tell her the awful things he'd done. The thought twisted his gut, but he knew it was the right thing to do.

For her sake, not his.

When she'd apologized for kissing him, he'd choked on his coffee. If anyone should apologize, it should be him.

As if he didn't do his part in feasting on the sweetness she'd offered.

Taking his frustration out on the log he was chopping helped. The physical labor warmed his muscles and helped clear his mind. After spending another bad night in his tent, he wondered if maybe he should simply pack up and head out of town, forgetting the invitation to visit Ian over Christmas. Getting close to people, especially Raven and Ian, was messing with his head.

What if he did something awful again? Or was this a sign he was finally getting better?

He was afraid to believe the latter.

When he'd finished half the log, he lowered the ax and drew in a deep breath. Lifting his gaze to the cloudy sky, he tried a quick prayer for the first time in his life.

Show me the way.

He propped the ax against the woodpile, then headed up to the cabin. As he reached the door, it opened, revealing Raven standing there. She was dressed in a bright blue sweater, one that emphasized the color of her eyes, and a pair of figure-hugging blue jeans. Her dark hair was long and shiny, and he had to close his fingers into fists to keep from burying his hands deep in her lovely hair.

She was so beautiful she took his breath away.

"I hope you're hungry," she said, opening the door wide for him to come in. "I have lots of eggs and bacon too. I didn't start the eggs because I wasn't sure how you liked them."

"Any way is fine." It wasn't easy to speak past the tightness of his throat. Entering the cabin had felt almost like coming home. Which was nuts.

He didn't have a home.

"Make what you like," he said when she continued looking at him expectantly.

"Over easy with toast?" She flashed a grin.

"That's my favorite."

Warning sirens went off in the back of his mind. He shouldn't be here. With her.

He liked Raven, too much.

Yet his body refused to leave.

"Over easy is great." Belle jumped up, distracting him. The tightness of his throat eased as he stroked the puppy.

If he didn't live such a nomadic life, he'd consider getting a dog of his own. But that wouldn't be fair, especially when food was scarce.

And the winter weather brutal.

What was with him wanting things he couldn't have? He'd been perfectly content roaming the countryside with nothing but his own thoughts for comfort.

And the occasional odd job to buy food and other necessities.

"Jack? Take your coat off and stay awhile."

He flushed and gently set Belle aside. Steeling his resolve to put an end to this romantic fantasy once and for all, he shrugged out of his coat and set it near the wood-burning stove. By habit, he checked it to make sure he didn't need to add more wood, then he noticed the Christmas fabric spread out on her quilt table.

"I thought you were working on a yellow and blue quilt?"

She glanced at him over her shoulder. "I stopped at Carla's craft store yesterday and found out she'd sold every single one of my Christmas quilts and had two more people who still wanted one. I guess they don't mind that the quilts won't be finished by Christmas."

"Ian's wife, Sarah, has one of your quilts." He came over to stand near the table. "She loves it and claims you do amazing work."

Raven blushed and smiled. "I'm glad to hear it, but I feel as if the sales will slack off eventually. I mean, how many quilts does one household need? Although I have done some baby quilts that are also big sellers."

He thought for a moment about Grace, the toddler on Sarah's hip, and the little boy, Ethan. It belatedly occurred to him that the kids, including Ben, were his nephews and niece.

He was their uncle.

"Sit down, Jack, the eggs are just about ready." She expertly flipped them and then brought the skillet over to the table where she'd set out two plates. She slid the over-easy eggs out, three for him and two for her.

He took his seat, then bowed his head, waiting for her prayer. She didn't disappoint.

"Dear Lord, thank You for this wonderful meal we're blessed to share today. We continue to ask for Your guidance as we follow Your chosen path. And thank You for healing Ian Kramer's leukemia. Amen."

"Amen." Jack was touched she'd included his brother. He picked up his fork and tried his eggs. Delicious. "Do you know anything about being a bone marrow transplant donor?"

Raven looked surprised by his question. "No, why? Does Ian need one?"

"Not now, but it's a possibility for the future." He glanced at her. "I'd like to be tested, but I'm not sure they'll take me."

"Why not?" Then she nodded. "Oh, I see. You mean because of the outstanding warrant?"

"Yeah." Among other things, but that was the biggest hurdle at the moment.

They ate in silence for a few minutes before Raven asked, "What does Ian think?"

"About me being a donor?"

"No, about your outstanding warrant." Her blue eyes were full of hope. "Isn't it possible that whatever you did before doesn't matter anymore?"

"Doubtful." He didn't want to ruin their breakfast, but she deserved to know.

And really, it was the best way for him to get out of here, once and for all. Because he didn't think he had the strength to refuse if Raven kept inviting him back.

"Maybe we can get you a fake name."

Her suggestion stopped him cold. Was she seriously offering to help shield him from his criminal past?

"Raven, please." He finished his eggs and bacon, pushed his plate aside, then forced himself to meet her gaze. "I need you to know how much I appreciate everything you've done for me. Inviting me in, giving me your trust has been incredible. But I'm not the man you think I am."

"I already told you, I don't care what you did in the past, Jack."

"That's because you have no idea what I've done." He really, really didn't want to tell her, but it was well past time she knew the truth. "First of all, my name isn't Jack Keller. It's Jesse Kramer."

"Of course, I should have figured that out. Great news too." He stared at her in confusion, wondering if she misunderstood. "You already have a fake name."

Seriously? She was happy about that? He couldn't stand her kindness a moment longer.

"I almost killed a man, a woman, and their dog." The statement was blunt and to the point. He glanced where Belle and Sadie were stretched out on the floor.

The light in her eyes died.

"I also started a forest fire that could have killed hundreds." He swallowed hard. "I can't say I remember the details, everything is fuzzy. In my mind, they were hostiles and prevented me from living off the land. As I mentioned, I was in a dark place back then, but that's no excuse for my behavior. After jail, I was placed in a psychiatric facility, which was just the same as jail, but with different colors on the walls. I escaped and never looked back."

Raven continued looking at him as if she'd never seen him before. And he understood where she was coming from.

She romanticized what they'd shared. This brief interlude from reality.

He abruptly stood, reached for his coat, and headed toward the door.

"Jack, wait!" Raven's protest was weak.

Every cell in his body wanted to turn around and hope to see something other than disgust, or worse, fear in her eyes.

But he was too much of a coward.

He left, closing the door with a firm click.

Leaving what was left of his heart behind.

9

R aven jumped out of her chair, wincing as she placed her weight on her injured ankle. She grabbed the cane and hobbled after Jack.

But by the time she managed to pull the cabin door open, the area was empty.

"Jack!" She called his name several times, listening carefully for a response. All was quiet. He was long gone, or would be very soon, and she couldn't follow in an attempt to track him down. Hiking through the woods on her gimpy ankle with the cane for support was only asking for trouble.

Belle and Sadie came over to stand beside her in the doorway, but she prevented them from going out. "Stay."

Belle, of course, didn't listen, darting in and out of the cabin in confusion, but Sadie must have sensed her despair because the shepherd stayed close to her side.

Easing back, she closed the cabin door with a terrible sense of finality. After making her way back to the kitchen table, she sank into her seat and stared at the empty place across from her. At some level, she wished she would have asked Josie for the gossip around Ian's brother Jack, or rather, Jesse. If she'd have known the details of his crimes ahead of time, she could have tempered her reaction.

She thought she'd been prepared to hear Jack's history, feeling certain it had been something like driving under the influence or maybe a physical altercation with someone.

But threatening to kill people? And a dog? Setting the fire that had taken out a big chunk of the land? She'd remembered being upset when the fire had happened.

She'd never imagined Jack had anything to do with that.

Especially since he'd been sweet, kind, caring, and supportive since the day they'd first met.

He'd made her a Christmas wreath. The cane was practical, as was stacking the wood near her door, but the wreath was a sweet gesture, done only for the purpose of giving her joy and happiness.

Which didn't jibe with what he'd done. She couldn't wrap her mind around it. None of it made any sense.

She dropped her head in her hands and called herself every kind of fool. Jack had suffered from PTSD, probably still did. He'd mentioned there were problems with his ability to be around people.

And those problems had been far worse than she'd thought.

She told herself that people could change. That God had given up his own son to forgive their sins, which included those belonging to Jack.

Surely as she was sitting here, the man had changed over the past few years. Everyone changed. She wasn't the same woman now as the day she lost Daniel.

If only she hadn't reacted so badly. She felt certain that, deep down, Jack had been hoping and searching for a second chance.

One she waited a heartbeat too long to give.

Sadie rested her head on Raven's lap as if she, too, missed Jack. And when Belle tried to jump up to join them, she cuddled the puppy close, trying hard not to cry.

Raven didn't allow herself to wallow in her sorrows for long. She'd always known Jack wasn't going to stay. What did it matter if he left now or in a couple of days?

Gone was gone.

And she had work to do.

Raven made wild turkey soup from the turkey bones and leftover meat, in honor of Jack's last present to her, before heading over to her sewing machine and quilt table.

She had orders to fill. And new quilt designs to make.

This was her life—the one God had chosen for her.

It was up to her to make the most of His gifts.

∼

JACK HAD WALKED for a long time before making a loop and returning to his camp about thirty yards from Raven's cabin. The stinging disappointment of Raven's response had faded, leaving a grim resolve in its place. Her reaction to the news was exactly what he'd expected. There was absolutely no reason to feel let down.

She had made a life for herself here. Had been doing very well on her own, making quilts and breeding Sadie. She was tough and independent.

He was just a drifter passing through.

Kneeling near a large tree, he pulled out his binoculars. Focusing the lens, he swept the area around the trip wires for new footprints.

But found nothing.

Had he overreacted to the footprints he'd discovered? Sadie had growled but hadn't gone crazy barking or trying to track anyone.

The intruder had likely been long gone by that point anyway.

He considered the two possible suspects she'd mentioned, the dog guy, Taylor Wilkes, and the craft guy, Sean Calloway. Two men who had good reasons to be angry with her.

Jack considered hiking back to Ian's place to ask his brother to check both of them out, see if there were any red flags in their backgrounds.

The irony of this request wasn't lost on him, after all, his background held nothing but red flags.

He felt certain the intruder wouldn't be back until dark, so he broke down his camp and retraced his path from yesterday, returning to Ian and Sarah's home.

Oddly enough, it didn't feel like the place where he and Ian had grown up. In some way, his life had been bifurcated into two parts: pre-Afghanistan and post-Afghanistan.

He'd never be the man he was before his last tour overseas. He couldn't even mourn that man because he was dissected from his previous life. The hours of torture he'd endured had wreaked havoc on his mind.

A quick glance up toward the sky had him wondering about God. About how Jack had been driven to return to Crystal Lake, Wisconsin, even though he'd never planned to come back.

Because God had chosen this path for him? In response to Ian's and Sarah's prayers?

He sent up a silent request for God to watch over Raven in his absence, relieved she had both Sadie and the puppy for company.

The temperature had dropped a good ten degrees from the day before, well below freezing, so he could see his breath in the air. Hiking at a steady pace kept him warm.

When he arrived at Ian's place, he hesitated, wondering how his brother and his wife would feel about a second unannounced visit. Normal people called ahead on their cell phone to make sure it was a good time to drop by.

He didn't have a cell phone.

And it hadn't occurred to him until this very moment that dropping in unannounced might be considered rude.

This was why he didn't belong here. Not here, in the woods, but living among civilized human beings.

He'd been a Big Foot nomad for too long.

"Uncle Jesse?"

He spun around so quickly he almost fell, startled to hear his real name. His gaze focused on the boy, Ben.

"Hi." He forced a smile so the kid wouldn't run into the house screaming in fear. "Ben, right? You must be about nine or ten now."

"Ten," Ben confirmed. "My mom told me that you helped us escape when my dad tried to kidnap us."

Why in the world would Sarah tell this boy about that? "I, uh, yeah. I helped."

Ben's expression was solemn. "I remember being so scared we were going to die. But then my dad tripped and fell, and my dad, my real dad, came to rescue us." The boy tipped his head to the side as if regarding him carefully. "Mom said you set wires along the ground to trip him and disabled his car so he couldn't drive us away."

"Yeah, well." He had no idea what to say to this boy who had eyes like a man. "I'm glad I could help."

"Thank you," Ben said simply. The boy glanced back at the house. "I love my real dad and my brother and sister, although Ethan always messes with my stuff."

A reluctant grin tugged at the corner of his mouth. For a rare second, he remembered the way he and Ian would fight over the exact same thing. "I used to get into your dad's stuff too. When we were kids."

"Mom and Dad were hoping you'd come back, but it's not Christmas yet."

"No, I, uh, wanted to talk to your dad for a minute. If he has time."

Ben nodded eagerly. "Sure, he's got time. Come on, I'll take you in."

Jack followed Ben around to the front of the house. Ian was outside and about to start up the snowblower.

"I'll do that for you," he offered. "Just show me how to run it."

"I need to do it to build up my strength," Ian said. He gave Jack a one-armed hug. "Glad to see you again so soon, bro."

Jack felt a little guilty that he'd come with an ulterior motive. "I need a favor, Ian. There are a couple of guys that might be bothering Raven, and I was hoping you could do a background check to see if there's a reason for me to worry."

Ian lifted a brow. "Okay, sure. Come inside and I'll take a look."

Jack followed Ian inside, setting his pack on the floor next to the door, surprised to see that a large Christmas tree had been put up since the last time he'd been there.

Wasn't that just yesterday?

He edged closer, searching for the familiar family ornaments. There were two, one with each of their childhood photos in them, both taken when they were about Ben's age.

And there they were, not just Ian's childhood ornament, but his too. The one he'd left at the top of the tree four years ago in a silent message to his brother that he'd been there.

Ian had kept it all these years, placing it on the tree in his honor.

"I've been praying for you, Jesse," Ian murmured, having come up to stand beside him. "When I was sick, my prayers turned a little selfish, I wanted the chance to see you one last time. But what I mostly prayed for is that you would find peace."

Jack nodded. "I did." Why didn't Raven have a tree? She'd hung his wreath on the wall, but it just occurred to him now that she hadn't put up a Christmas tree.

"I can tell." Ian clapped him on the back. "Come over to the computer. I need the names of these two guys you're interested in."

He followed Ian to the kitchen counter and the laptop computer sitting there. Sarah was baking something that smelled really good, apple pie? He shouldn't be hungry after Raven's breakfast, but that didn't stop him from sniffing the air with appreciation.

"Taylor Wilkes and Sean Calloway," he said as Ian worked the computer. "I'm not entirely sure of the spelling."

"Any date of birth?"

"No." He frowned, hoping that wasn't a deterrent.

Ian tried a few names and found something on Taylor Wilkes. "Looks like Taylor likes to fight, there's a restraining order against him from an old girlfriend, and he has an assault and battery charge too."

"Raven's instincts were right about him." Jack peered over Ian's shoulder. "But nothing on Sean Calloway?"

"No." Ian shrugged. "Let's take a short drive

into town, check with HQ. They may know something we don't."

Jack's instinct was to refuse, getting close to those who wanted to slap cuffs around his wrists wasn't high on his list of things to do, but concern for Raven won out. "Okay."

"I'll do the talking," Ian assured him. "And we'll introduce you as Jack Keller. No one will remember you from four years ago."

Jack wasn't sure about that but picked up his pack and headed out after Ian. Ben used the snowblower to make a path from the house to the driveway.

"Be careful, son," Ian warned. "Your mom will never forgive me if you lose a finger."

Ben rolled his eyes. "You say that every time, and I haven't been stupid enough to put my hand in there yet."

"I know, but still be careful, okay?"

When they were settled in Ian's Jeep, Jack glanced back at Ben. "He's a good kid, thanks to you."

"Thanks to you, Jesse." Ian flashed a grin. "It was a team effort."

He was touched to be included. Ian's Jeep ate up the miles, and they arrived at the sheriff's department headquarters within fifteen minutes.

Walking into the official police building made him tense. They passed a skinny guy who'd come out through the doorway, muttering to himself. Jack tried to look innocent but felt as if guilt was written all over his face in permanent ink for all to see.

Ian went straight back to where one of the

deputies was sitting. "Hey, Dev. I understand Raven Clark filed a complaint yesterday?"

"Yep." Devon Armbruster eyed Jack curiously. "She gave me the names of two possible perps."

"Taylor Wilkes and Sean Calloway," Ian said. "Seems Taylor has a rap sheet."

"A couple of pops from last year," Devon agreed. "Calloway came up clean though. Guy's cranky, no doubt about it, but I think he's harmless."

"Who was that guy who just left?" Jack asked.

"Brian Flynn, one of the mechanics at Billy's Auto Repair. Hank called the cops late last night because Brian was acting goofy, talking about women and complaining about birds." Devon shrugged. "Spent the night in jail for a disorderly, we just let him go."

"Okay, well maybe you guys can send a squad past her place on occasion, just in case," Ian was saying.

"Will do."

They walked back outside and climbed back into the Jeep. As his brother drove out of the parking lot, it hit him. Birds? He reached over to grab Ian's arm. "We need to get to Raven's place."

"Why?"

"Birds. Women and birds. Raven. We need to check it out."

Ian's expression turned grim. "You think Brian was going off about Raven?"

"Maybe. Let's hurry. Turn right, we have to head out of town in the opposite direction of your place."

"Maybe we should call Devon," Ian said, hitting the gas and following his directions.

Jack didn't want to waste a minute. "Call him but keep driving."

Ian used a computer screen in his dashboard to make the call, something Jack wasn't at all familiar with. Devon agreed to head out to meet with them, but Jack wasn't willing to wait.

The knot of fear in his gut tightened when he saw a black four-wheel truck parked along the side of the road in the exact same spot where he'd found the previous tire tracks.

"That's him," Jack said, an eerie calm settling over him. He didn't wait for Ian to come to a complete stop but pushed open the passenger side door and jumped out, hitting the ground in a sprint.

"Jesse, wait!"

"I'm going in through the back," he shot over his shoulder. "You take the front."

Ignoring everything else, Jack focused on rounding the cabin to the back of Raven's cabin. He hoped and prayed, seriously prayed, that they'd gotten there in time. That Raven would be okay and he'd find Brian Flynn flat on his face from the trip wires.

But there was no sign of anyone in the snow in the space between the cabin and the garage. Easing up to the cabin's back door, he tested the door and nearly wept in relief when he found it unlocked.

Stealthily easing inside, he crept along the back hallway, toward the living area. His blood ran cold as he heard their voices.

"Brian, please understand, I think you're a wonderful guy. But the gun in your hand is making me nervous. Put it down and we'll have coffee and talk, okay?"

Gun? Jack only had his knife in the sheath on his hip, not a gun.

His heart thudded painfully against his ribs. If Brian hurt one hair on Raven's head, Jack wasn't sure he'd be able to hold himself back from killing him.

10

———

Raven stared down Brian Flynn with false bravado, her mind whirling. Her only weapon was Sadie, and if she gave her dog the command to attack, she feared he'd shoot and kill her.

Belle too.

As she watched the clearly unbalanced man who'd initially asked for help, then started brandishing a gun, she realized she should have taken Jack's concerns more seriously. She'd given him the names of Taylor Wilkes and Sean Calloway as possible suspects, but she had never even mentioned her strange interaction with Brian. Apparently, the poor guy was under the delusion that having waited the respectful year plus a few months after Daniel's death, he was free to claim her as his own.

Despite the fact that she didn't want anything to do with him.

Belle let out a couple of sharp barks, making Raven wince.

"Shut that dog up!" Brian shouted. "Or I'll shut him up for you."

"Shh, Belle, sit. Stay." Raven kept a hand on the back of Sadie's neck, feeling the tension radiating through the animal. The dog had picked up on her fear and would attack Brian at the slightest command, but at what cost? A gunshot wound?

Raven couldn't do it.

Belle continued to whine, the puppy's gaze focused on the hallway leading to the two bedrooms and bathroom. It was the same whining sound Belle had made sitting in front of the door after Jack had left.

A sliver of hope bloomed in her chest. Was it possible Jack had come back? If anyone could get her out of this mess, it was him.

But she needed to distract Brian before he realized they weren't alone. "Are you sure you don't want coffee, Brian? Or how about some turkey soup? I bet you're hungry." Raven forced a smile. "I made fresh bread today. Please, join me for lunch."

Brian eyed her with suspicion. "Does this mean you're willing to be my woman?"

The question put her teeth on edge. "If that's what you want, then yes." It was difficult to say the words without showing her extreme distaste. "But I don't think men hold their women at gunpoint, do they?"

Brian seemed to consider this and nodded. "Okay, fine. I won't need the gun as long as you behave, Raven."

The minute he lowered the gun, she shouted, "Get him!"

Sadie leaped forward, a quivering mass of muscle and teeth. Out of nowhere, Jack hurtled forward, grabbing Brian's gun hand and twisting his wrist with enough force that she was afraid he'd snapped his arm in two.

The gun hit the floor with a heavy thud. Jack kicked it across the room. Brian howled in pain as Sadie planted her front feet on his chest and barked in his face, her teeth nipping at his nose.

"Call her off," he wailed. "She bit me!"

"Come, Sadie," Raven said. "Sadie!"

The dog dropped to all fours, still growling as Jack wrenched Brian's arm behind his back and forced him down onto his knees. Jack's stony expression gave her pause, but then her front door burst open. Deputy Armbruster rushed inside, followed by Ian Kramer.

"What happened?" Devon asked, holding his gun pointed at Brian.

"H-he wanted to claim me as his woman," Raven said shakily. "He threatened me and my dogs at gunpoint, told me everything would be okay as long as I behaved."

"Idiot," Devon muttered. "Brian Flynn, you're under arrest for assault with a deadly weapon." Devon clapped silver handcuffs around the guy's wrists as he howled in pain. Brian continued to babble, talking to himself in a way that was downright scary.

Devon looked up. "Jesse, you can let go now."

Jack and Ian gaped at him in surprise at the sound of Jack's real name. Jack backed off, his gaze darting toward the rear of the cabin as if ready to run.

"What, do you think I'm some sort of idiot that I don't recognize the family resemblance between you? You share the same green eyes." Devon shook his head wryly. "Don't worry, your secret is safe with me. Nice work bringing this guy down, Jesse. Appreciate the assist."

Raven took a step toward Jack, but Belle, of course, beat her to him. The puppy joyfully jumped up in an attempt to lick his face. Jack hesitated for a tenuous moment, then slowly lowered to one knee to scoop the puppy into his arms.

"You almost gave me away, Belle," he chided in that low husky voice of his. "Good thing Brian here was clueless enough not to notice."

Raven crossed over to Jack. "I prayed you'd come back in time."

Jack lifted his green gaze to hers. "I prayed I'd get here in time. I'm sorry I wasn't here when you needed me."

"Your timing was perfect." Although the minutes she'd spent trying to talk Brian down had seemed to drag on for an eternity. "Better late than never, right?"

He rubbed Belle, then stood. He was close enough to touch, and she wanted nothing more than to be in his arms. But she held back, remembering that she'd initiated their first and only kiss.

What happened next had to be his decision.

She mentally prepared herself for the worst. For Jack to turn and walk away, this time for good. But he reached for her hand and tugged her close.

"Oh, Jack," she murmured.

He didn't respond, but simply lowered his head and kissed her.

Raven's heart sang with joy as he stole her breath and deepened their kiss. She clutched his shoulders, her knees going weak. Or maybe it was her bum ankle threatening to give way. It was difficult to think while Jack was kissing her as if he'd never stop.

When Jack finally ended their kiss, she tightened her grip on his shoulders, not wanting to let go. "Please stay," she whispered. "Here. With me. At least for a while." It was pathetic to know that she'd take whatever scrap of attention he had to give.

He stared into her eyes, his expression full of desire and regret. His hands tightened on her waist. "What I want and what I should do are very different. I can't drag you down with me, Raven. I won't."

She glanced over her shoulder to see that Devon had taken Brian out of the cabin to his squad, leaving Ian there, grinning at them. "Did Deputy Armbruster really mean that about his secret being safe?"

"Yes." Ian's simple answer filled her with hope. "I believe in second chances, Jesse. Don't you?"

Jack hesitated, clearly torn. "It's not right to escape the punishment I deserve."

Ian considered that for a moment. "Okay, but don't you think your self-imposed punishment was strict enough? How many guys in prison would be able to live off the land with nothing but a fifty-pound pack for six months, let alone four long years? I'm willing to say not a single one."

Jack seemed unconvinced.

"And don't forget you've done good things

during your isolation," Ian continued. "Like helping me find Sarah and Ben, and again with Raven. I think the good you've done outweighs the bad. And you rehabilitated yourself without costing the state a dime. That must count for something."

Jack shrugged but didn't respond. His silence was unnerving.

"At least stay for lunch," Raven pressed, hoping that more time together might change Jack's mind. "Ian, you're welcome to stay too."

"Oh, I wouldn't want to be a third wheel here," Ian teased. "See you later, bro."

Ian walked out, closing the cabin door behind him.

Raven could have hugged Ian for leaving them alone. Now if she could only find a way to convince Jack to stay.

Not just for lunch, but longer. Through the holidays, Christmas and New Year's.

Maybe forever.

~

Jack couldn't believe Devon and Ian had simply left him here alone with Raven. Especially Devon.

He'd fully expected to feel the bite of handcuffs around his wrists too.

"Thanks for coming to my rescue." Raven wrapped her arms around his neck.

Kissing her was something he could get used to, but his situation was serious. Why was she taking it so lightly? He lowered his head until his forehead rested on hers. "Raven, I'm not sure what to do here."

"Why don't we pray about it?"

He jerked his head up in surprise. "Pray?"

"It's not a foreign concept, Jack." She smiled and captured both of his hands in hers. She brought them up between them, her eyes never leaving his. "Dear Lord, please guide us on Your chosen path," she began.

"While keeping us safe from harm," Jack added.

"We ask for strength and for light so that we may do Your will."

"Amen," Jack said. He let out a soundless sigh, feeling as if he'd run a marathon. "I've never prayed out loud before."

"God is always listening, whether we pray silently or out loud." She cupped his bearded cheek with her hand. "God loves you, Jack. I believe he brought you to Crystal Lake for a reason."

"I want to believe that too." The reason was Ian's illness, but maybe his stumbling across Raven was another part of God's plan too.

Should he stay or should he go? How was he supposed to know what God had in mind?

"Listen to your heart," Raven said as if reading his mind. "If nothing else mattered, other than you and me, your brother, his wife, and their children, what would you do?"

"I'd stay." The words popped out of his mouth before he could even think about them. A slow warmth spread through his chest, and he realized that maybe, just maybe he was on the right track. Still, the memory of how she'd reacted to his past concerned him. "But what about you? I know you were horrified to learn what I'd done. And I understand. I don't blame you for that, Raven."

"That was four years ago," Raven said firmly. "And I think Ian is right. You spent the past four years in a jail of your own making. Of self-imposed isolation. Don't you think you've punished yourself enough?"

"I—don't know." What was the going rate for setting a fire and almost killing innocent people? He didn't think four years was even close to long enough.

"God has forgiven you, Jack." Raven stared into his eyes. "Don't you think it's time you forgive yourself?"

He wanted to believe there was something more for him than continuing to trek aimlessly across the country. A novel concept since he had never had a plan to do anything else, until now.

"I think the better question is whether or not you can forgive me?"

"Me?" She looked surprised. "Why wouldn't I forgive you? Jack Jesse Kramer Keller, don't you realize I'm falling in love with you?"

Love? Whoa, he had never expected that. His instincts screamed at him to take a step back, but as if sensing his intent, she slid her hand around to the back of his neck, holding him in place.

"I love you," she repeated. "I know it sounds crazy, we barely know each other, but that doesn't seem to matter. My heart knows what it wants, and it wants you."

The last of his stubborn resolve crumbled to dust. "I love you too, Raven." He pulled her close and kissed her again. "And those are words I've never said to another woman."

"Then I'm honored to be the first," she said with a smile.

He wanted to kiss her again but forced himself to show some restraint. He might be a Neanderthal Big Foot, but he would not do anything to harm Raven. Including ruining her reputation.

Not now, not ever.

"Ah, did you mention something about having turkey soup for lunch?"

Raven laughed. "Yes, I did. And trust me, I did not want to share it with Brian Flynn."

He went still, thinking of those moments when he'd nearly broken Flynn's arm. "I was worried I'd be too late. And if he'd hurt you . . ." He didn't finish, unable to verbalize his deepest fear.

"You wouldn't have," Raven said with utmost confidence.

"How do you know?"

"Because God would have stopped you."

He swallowed hard. "Stopped me from doing what?"

"From hurting him."

The revelation was humbling. Was that really true? God had guided him back to Crystal Lake, so she could be right. Anything was possible.

And in a way, it was also reassuring. He decided then and there to do his best to be the kind of man Raven thought he was.

But there was one last thing bothering him. "Raven, is there a reason you don't have a Christmas tree?"

She shrugged. "I wasn't planning to celebrate

the holiday, except maybe by reading the Bible. A tree doesn't mean much when you don't have anyone to share it with."

"I'd like to have a tree." He wanted the same cheeriness for Raven as he'd seen at Ian's. "We can make ornaments if you don't have any."

"I have some stored away in the basement." A hesitant smile brightened her features. "We can find a tree after lunch, then spend the afternoon decorating it."

"I like that plan." He couldn't believe he was actually looking forward to the holiday.

"Let the dogs out while I get lunch ready."

"Okay, but I think Sadie deserves a treat for her heroic rescue."

"Here, Sadie," Raven called, taking something from the fridge. Sadie's tail swished back and forth with excitement as Raven offered her a piece of turkey.

Sadie swallowed it in one gulp, making him smile.

Belle was vying for his attention, so he bent down to stroke the puppy, then took both dogs outside. His pack was leaning up against the door. Ian must have taken it from the Jeep and left it there for him.

He thought about Ian and Sarah and their invitation to share Christmas together.

Glancing back at the cabin, he knew they wouldn't mind if he brought Raven along.

In fact, they'd likely be mad if he didn't.

As he approached the cabin, it occurred to him that he hadn't felt this comfortable in an enclosed space in years.

A sign of healing. His PTSD wouldn't go away completely, it would always remain a part of him, but he didn't have the same level of nightmares he'd once had.

And maybe Raven was right about learning to forgive himself for what he'd done.

He'd made mistakes, had hurt innocent people with his threats of harm and starting the fire. Why God had given him this second chance, he wasn't sure, but he didn't dare waste it.

He called the dogs, and they came bounding inside the cabin. Closing the door behind them, he noticed Raven had set two places at the kitchen table.

Right next to each other, rather than across from each other.

The bowls were full of tasty turkey noodle soup, and there were slices of fresh bread. He washed his hands and took the seat beside her.

Raven held her hand out for his. He took it and knew better than to sit quietly this time.

This woman he loved liked to pray out loud. Something he figured he'd better get accustomed to.

"Dear Lord, we thank You for this wonderful meal You've provided for us," he said, echoing her previous prayers.

She tightened her grip on his hand. "We thank You for keeping us safe from harm, and we ask You to heal Brian Flynn's illness."

"We ask that You continue to guide us on Your chosen path. Amen," he finished.

"Amen," Raven added. She didn't let go of his hand. "Jack? I love you so much."

For the first time in his memory, tears pricked at his eyes. "I love you too, Raven."

His heart swelled with the knowledge that God had brought him here to Raven.

A place he could call home.

EPILOGUE

C hristmas Day
Raven was thrilled to spend Christmas with Ian, Sarah, and their three children, Ben, Grace, and Ethan. She brought fresh bread because she didn't have much to offer.

Sarah didn't seem to mind, gratefully taking the bread and waving Raven toward the living room. "Go, sit, relax. How is your ankle, by the way?"

"Almost back to normal." She couldn't deny a twinge of regret that Jack had no reason to carry her around anymore. "Are you sure I can't help you with something?"

"Dinner won't be ready for another hour or so," Sarah said. "I promised the kids they could open their presents while we wait."

Raven nodded. "Okay." Jack had been working on carving gifts for his nephews and niece while she worked on her quilts. He'd kept them a secret, so she wasn't sure what to expect.

She entered the living room, and Jack immediately waved her over. Sadie was lying on the floor with the kids, but Jack had Belle in his lap. The puppy adored Jack and obeyed his commands in a way that made it clear she belonged to him. After feeling put out at first, Raven decided she was okay with that. If anyone deserved a dog of his own, it was Jack. He took her hand, drawing her down to sit beside him.

There was no place she'd rather be.

"Okay, you can open some of your presents," Sarah said, drawing little Grace into her lap. "Ladies first."

"Aw, Mom," Ethan protested.

"Always," Ian agreed. "Go on, Grace, open your gift from Uncle Jack."

Ian and Sarah had been calling Jack by the name on his driver's license as a way to protect him. Although Ian had confided in Jack that he'd already spoken to Sheriff Torretti about Jesse's outstanding warrant. Sheriff Torretti had pretended to know nothing about it, and Ian couldn't find evidence of the warrant either.

Maybe the Sheriff, who was also a believer and a churchgoing man, had also decided Jack deserved a second chance.

Grace pulled the Christmas cloth bag open and pulled out a beautifully carved puppy, one that looked just like Belle. "My doggy," she exclaimed, then put it up to her mouth. Thankfully, it was too big to swallow.

"Say thank you to Uncle Jack."

Grace hid her face against her mother. "Tank you."

"You're welcome."

"Me next!" Ethan ripped open his Christmas cloth. "A bear," he said in awe.

"They hibernate in winter, but you'll catch glimpses of them in the spring," Jack explained. "Just make sure you stay far away, especially if there are cubs around."

"Your uncle made that out of wood with his own hands," Ian told his son. "You can imagine how long that took."

Ethan nodded and grinned. "Thanks, Uncle Jack!"

"Dad, is it okay if I open mine now?" Ben asked.

"Of course," Ian responded.

Ben took his time, his eyes widening with excitement when he saw the carving. "A cougar!"

"It's rare to see them in nature, but I've had the pleasure of watching them from afar. They are beautiful animals."

Raven knew that cougars held a special place in Jack's heart. He'd been protecting a cougar all those years ago. It didn't end well, his mind playing tricks on him, but his initial goal had been on target.

"You're the best, Uncle Jack." Ben thumped Jack's shoulder in the universal way men showed gratitude toward each other. "Thanks."

"There's one more there, for Raven," Jack said.

"Me?" Raven stared in surprise. No wonder he'd kept his carvings a secret. She opened the bag with her name on it and smiled when she pulled out the carving of a rooster. "I love it, Jack, thank you."

"There's something else." He handed her a

folded sheet of paper. She opened it and frowned at the drawing he'd sketched. "What's this?"

"Your chicken coop. I'll start building it in the spring."

"But—it's huge!" The drawing made the chicken coop look bigger than her entire cabin.

"Well, there's a greenhouse too." Jack flushed and shrugged. "Figured we'll need a bigger garden."

"We will?" The way he included himself in his plans was heartwarming. He'd insisted on sleeping outside at night as a way to protect her honor, but they'd spent the past few days together.

Jack pulled a small circular object from his pocket. It was a ring carved out of wood, and he held it out to her. "I don't have enough money for a proper engagement ring, so this was the best I could do." He hesitated, then added, "Raven, will you marry me?"

Ian, Sarah, and the kids all gaped in surprise. Raven held out her hand so he could slide the ring onto her finger. "Yes, Jack, I'll marry you." She thought about his sleeping outside. "The sooner the better."

"I love you, and I like the way you think." He kissed her.

"Congratulations, Jack and Raven," Ian said with a broad smile. "You know, Pastor John will be happy to perform a small ceremony for you both, likely with few questions asked."

"That would be wonderful," Raven admitted.

"Yes, very much so," Jack murmured. Then he cleared his throat and looked at the kids. "Okay, who's next to open a present?"

"Me!" all three kids exclaimed at once.

Everyone laughed and offered their congratulations. Raven held Jesse's carving close to her heart, knowing that God hadn't just brought Jack home for Christmas.

He'd brought Jack home forever.

IF YOU ENJOYED CHRISTMAS REDEMPTION:

You'll want to check out all six books of "Puppies for Christmas"! These are all **unconnected** Christmas stories you'll enjoy by authors you'll come to love and all priced at $0.99 until January 1, 2021:

Beneath Northern Lights - Lyn Cote - https://booksbylyncote.com/SWBS/books-by-lyn/beneath-northern-lights-a-holiday-story

The Mistletoe Puppy - by Roxanne Rustand - My Book

Christmas Redemption - By Laura Scott

Puppy Love and Jingle Bells by Merrillee Whren - https://www.merrilleewhren.com/book/puppy-love-and-jingle-bells/

Joy Comes to Bedford Falls - Susan Aylworth - My Book

A Christmas Puppy to Cherish - Josie Rivera - https://mybook.to/ChristmasPuppyCherish

I hope you enjoyed Jack and Raven's story in *Christmas Redemption*. Ever since I finished writing *Christmas Reunion*, I found myself thinking of Jesse Kramer and where he might be today. A very helpful reader mentioned I should write his story, and suddenly I couldn't wait to do just that.

I am very blessed to have such wonderful readers! Reviews are very important to authors, so if you liked *Christmas Redemption*, I would very much appreciate you taking the time to write a review.

I adore hearing from my readers! I can be contacted through Facebook at https://www.facebook.com/LauraScottBooks/ and on Twitter at https://twitter.com/laurascottbooks. I can also be reached through my website at https://www.laurascottbooks.com. Take a moment to subscribe to my newsletter, I offer a free Crystal Lake novella *Starting Over* to all subscribers. This novella is not available for sale on any format, it is exclusive only to those of you who sign up.

Lastly, if you haven't read my Christian international thriller book, *Target For Terror*, you may want to give it a try. I have included the first chapter here for your reading pleasure.

Yours in faith,
Laura Scott

June 30 – 7:06 p.m. – *Washington, DC*

"I saw the man who shot me."

Natalia Sokolova heard the words in rapid Russian, the language of her birth, and glanced in surprise at her patient. Her fingers faltered in the process of hanging the second unit of blood on his IV pump.

"Are you sure?" she responded in Russian.

Josef Korolev nodded, his gaze boring into hers. "The FBI agent in the front row of the crowd shot me."

What? An FBI agent shot him? "That can't be. You must be mistaken."

"*Eto ne oshibk*. There was no mistake." The deputy prime minister of Russia's voice was hoarse, scratchy because of the breathing tube that had been removed just a short while ago. "I saw him."

She finished connecting the unit of blood, then placed a reassuring hand on his arm. The deputy prime minister had come to Washington, DC, to deliver a speech regarding the importance of the Middle East Peace Summit to take place at the International Conference scheduled in Moscow. During the speech he'd been shot, which had caused quite the international incident. The entire country was in an uproar over the event.

Josef Korolev grabbed her hand as if willing her to believe him. "Listen to me. I saw him. The bullet came from close range. They didn't think I'd live long enough to tell."

He spoke with such heartfelt conviction the ugly shadow of doubt was difficult to ignore. Especially given the tenuous relationship between the US and Russia. Could her patient be confused? Thinking back over the few hours since Josef had returned from the OR, she counted the amount of narcotics she'd given him. A total of ten milligrams of morphine wasn't too much for such a large man over a three-hour period. Obviously, Josef Korolev had been shot, the Secret Service agents standing guard outside his room substantiated that. But by an FBI agent? She seriously doubted it.

The rumor zipping through the hospital grapevine claimed some sort of disgruntled assassin from the Russian mob was the prime suspect in the shooting because the Russian government was losing its battle against the Mafia underworld. The hospital had cops stationed at each entrance and several more in the ICU.

Yet all the police in the world couldn't keep Korolev safe if the suspect was really an FBI agent.

No, she couldn't believe it. Likely, the morphine was too much for him.

"You're safe here," she assured him. "This is

the surgical intensive care unit at Washington University Hospital, and I'm your nurse, Natalia. There are two men from your country here with you, but they've stepped out to discuss arrangements for your transfer home. They'll be back soon."

"I am not safe. Will never be safe, not until I get back to Russia. You must help me." He was old enough to be her father, but his grip was strong as he clung desperately to her hand. "Do not leave me alone with anyone from the American government."

"I won't." She leaned over to pull his blanket up over his chest, knowing the blood transfusion would give him a chill.

"Where did you get this?" His gaze zeroed in on the two pendants dangling from around her neck. His heart rate jumped up, causing his monitor to alarm overhead, but she ignored the noise when he touched the crescent-shaped moon with the three amethyst stars pendant that hung above her Christian cross. "Who gave this to you?"

"My mother." The treasured pendant was the only item she possessed from her Russian birth mother. She would have explained more, but Josef had grown agitated, muttering something she couldn't quite make out, so she tucked the pendants underneath the collar of her scrubs. "Shh. Relax now."

Before Josef could say anything more, she noticed a trio of official-looking American men walking toward her patient's room. Natalia straightened, watching through the glass window as they paused to speak with the Secret Service agent and the Russian countrymen before entering. Instinctively, she took a step closer as if her mere presence would save Josef from harm.

"The deputy prime minister is awake?" The shortest of the three, a man whose FBI name tag identified him as T. Saunders, pinned her with a sharp gaze. "The breathing tube is out? He's able to answer questions?"

"Yes." She winced as Josef's hand grabbed hers and squeezed tightly to the point of bringing pain. She tried to smile. "Well, not really," she amended. "He's confused, speaking gibberish. The medication has strongly affected him."

The iron hold on her hand didn't ease at her words because Josef did not understand English. She bent close to her patient, speaking in Russian, "Shh, relax. I explained how you are too confused from the narcotics to discuss anything about the shooting right now."

Josef's grip on her hand subsided, and he closed his eyes, feigning sleep.

"You speak Russian too?" Saunders was clearly the leader of the three. The sneer on his face suggested he accused her of something vile.

"Yes, but only a little." Natalia forced a smile. "My adopted mother had dual citizenship in both Russia and here in the US. She taught me some basics of the language. But I'm afraid I have grown very rusty over the years since she passed away." After her adopted mother died, she continued to practice her Russian with her friend Ivan. Yet she couldn't explain the deep-seated certainty that she needed to downplay the extent of her knowledge of the Russian language.

"What exactly did he say to you?" Saunders persisted.

"I don't know, the words didn't make sense. I told you, he's confused. I've given him about ten milligrams of morphine."

"Maybe we need one of our own interpreters in here to tell us just how confused he is." Saunders's gaze challenged her opinion.

She schooled her features not to show her annoyance. "Please do. There is a Russian interpreter, Ivan Rasacovich, available through the hospital social service department if you are interested. As I mentioned, I am not an expert."

"It's a miracle he's survived the shooting," the tallest of the three commented as if to change the direction of the conversation and ease the tension in the room. He was the only one without an FBI name tag, his badge simply read visitor.

"Yeah, no thanks to you, Dreyer," Saunders said in a snide tone.

Dreyer's mouth tightened. "Or to any of us assigned to protect him. The whole event was a debacle, and we can't even get a clear view of the shootings from the cameras." His gaze swept back to the patient. "He's lucky the bullet missed his heart and only grazed his lung."

Natalia doubted Josef Korolev felt very lucky considering the lengthy surgical incision extending around the side of his chest, but she held her tongue. As the FBI agents argued about who might have wanted to silence the deputy prime minister, the man named Dreyer stared at her to the point he made her uncomfortable. He was younger than the others and not dressed in the traditional FBI garb consisting of black suit and matching tie. The simple black T-shirt, stretched across his taut chest, dark jacket, and slacks looked far too casual for an official visit. He might be described as handsome if you liked tall, dark-haired American men with square jaws and brilliant blue eyes.

Good thing she didn't. A broken heart had cured her of such foolishness. She preferred peace and quiet in her life compared to the never-ending drama of a so-called relationship.

"Please, I must ask you all to leave. It's time to change his dressing." Another blatant lie, but she didn't care. She didn't know who these men were or which person she could trust. There was no reason on earth for the FBI to shoot a Russian diplomat, especially while he happened to be ensconced in their protection, but she couldn't totally discount her patient's accusation either. Something wasn't quite right with this picture, and she wanted these men to go away because she didn't have time to waste figuring it out.

Her job was to provide nursing care to her patients. When the men simply stood there, she scowled. "The chest dressing needs to be changed. Would you rather I risk infection?"

"No, of course not." Dreyer nodded as if he completely understood. "We'll give you the privacy you need. Gentlemen?" He gestured toward the door.

The other two sent her hostile looks but, eventually, turned and left the room. Dreyer lingered. She tried not to squirm under his intense gaze.

"Natalia, do you also understand Ukrainian?"

His attempt at the language was stilted at best, and his tone was low as if he didn't want anyone to overhear.

At first she was suspicious when he used her name, then she realized she was wearing her hospital ID badge. She sniffed. Someone should tell the man his accent was terrible. "Not fluently, but enough to understand the basics," she answered in Ukrainian. Russian was very different from Ukrainian, a fact he should know. "Why do you ask?"

"No reason in particular. Good night, Natalia." The man turned and followed the others out of the room, leaving her to wonder what test she'd just taken.

And if she'd passed—or failed?

June 30 – 9:18 p.m. – Washington, DC

SHE DIDN'T GET much time alone with Josef from that point on, mostly because she was running back and forth helping one of her co-workers whose patient took a sudden turn for the worse. She had wanted to ask Josef about her pendant though, since he acted as if it were familiar. Had he seen one just like it? Did he perhaps know who designed the dainty Russian jewelry? The idea that her pendant might hold a clue to the true identity of her birth parents filled her with excitement. She couldn't wait to ask him more.

Natalia sat down at the workstation outside her patient's room to make a quick notation in

Josef's chart when a shrill triple-beeping sound grabbed her attention. Her gaze snapped from the computer to the blinking red alarm on the central bank of monitors.

Josef's heart rate had gone into a life-threatening arrhythmia.

"Call a code blue." Natalia jumped from her seat and dashed into the room, knocking aside the wide-eyed guard in her haste to reach her patient. V-tach without a pulse. She crawled up to kneel on the side of his bed to perform chest compressions.

The room flooded with medical staff who shoved the hovering Russian countrymen out of the way. Someone took over CPR while another began to give breaths with an Ambu bag.

"Shock him," the surgeon snapped.

Natalia was already slapping the defib patches onto his chest. She connected them to the defibrillator and twisted the knob to 200 joules. "All clear?" she asked before she administered a shock.

"Shock him again," Dr. Ventura ordered. She did as she was told, knowing the algorithm.

"Give him a third shock." All eyes in the room were on the monitor, hoping and praying for a conversion into a normal heart rhythm. But that didn't happen. "Continue CPR and give a bolus of amiodarone," the surgeon ordered. "Then start a drip."

Natalia injected the medication. She grabbed the drip prepared by the pharmacist on duty and hung it on the IV tubing. The surgeon continued to shout orders for labs, for more medication, and to place a breathing tube. They shocked the patient again, then one last time after another round of CPR. As a team, they labored over the patient for a good forty minutes, but despite their best efforts, his heart went into asystole.

Dr. Ventura, the surgeon who'd operated on Josef Korolev, finally shook his head and raised a hand. "Stop CPR. There's nothing more to do."

No! How had this happened? Her pulse raced from the adrenaline coursing through her system, yet she could only stare at the still, peaceful features of Josef Korolev. Less than three hours ago he'd spoken to her.

Now he was dead.

She put a hand to her chest as if to ease the pressure there. Dear Lord, she couldn't believe he was *dead*. Loud vocal protests from the Russian countrymen in the room ricocheted off the walls. Words of comfort failed her.

What could she say to them? She didn't know what had happened. Why had a stable patient suddenly gone into V-tach? Was there something she'd missed? She had several years of nursing experience, but no one was perfect. Yet, in retracing her actions during her shift, she could not think of a single thing she would have done differently. The only oddity, other than all the political hoopla of taking care of a VIP, had been the strange visit from the three Americans.

And Josef's wild accusations.

FBI and Secret Service agents swarmed the room. She stayed close, listening as they grilled the poor guard who'd been left on duty. When they'd finished with the guard, they turned their attention to her.

"Who else has access to this room, besides you?" the FBI agent named Wilcox asked in a harsh tone. "Was he left alone at all?"

"Most of the time he wasn't alone, the Russian countrymen were with him." Natalia glanced nervously between the two men. Why were they asking these questions? Did they honestly suspect something had been done to Josef intentionally?

Should she tell them what Josef had claimed? Yet, if his off-the-wall accusations were true, would telling the FBI help? Saunders and Bentley, the two men who'd come in with Dreyer, hadn't seemed at all sympathetic. She could easily imagine them protecting their own, especially given the political ramifications.

"Yeah, but they spent most of their time in the corner talking in low tones," the guard who'd been on duty said with disgust. "As if I could understand what they babbled about."

"Any member of the hospital staff would have access to his room," Natalia added. "But none of them would have come in unless it was to troubleshoot an alarm or respond to a call light. This isn't the first VIP we've taken care of."

"She wasn't in the room for the past forty minutes," the guard bailed her out. "The only person to come into the room was the housekeeping guy who cleaned the room." When twin sets of cold eyes stared at him, the guard shrugged. "Hey, I took his name—Ray Johnson—it's on the list. Johnson left the room about five minutes before the monitor alarmed."

The FBI agent turned back to her. "Do you know this housekeeper named Ray Johnson?"

"Of course I do." She frantically searched her memory, but she couldn't honestly remember seeing him at any time during her shift. A chill slid down her spine. "I don't remember seeing him around, but I was busy."

The two men exchanged a long glance. "What does he look like?"

"Tall, close to six feet, and very thin. Black hair, usually uncombed." She shrugged. It wasn't as if she knew the man on a personal basis, just enough to say hello.

"Caucasian?"

She nodded.

The guard frowned. "Sounds right, although I didn't think he was that tall, closer to five-ten or eleven. And his hair was more brown than black."

Wilcox, the FBI agent, turned toward the hospital security guard. "Pull up Ray Johnson's picture."

"I tried, but there's something wrong with the computer program." The security guard hunched his shoulders at their incredulous look. "They're working on it."

Wilcox muttered a curse.

Tiny hairs along her nape lifted in warning. *Stop it.* She gave her head a hard shake. Too many crime novels had gone straight to her head. There was no reason to let Josef's outrageous suspicions make her see something sinister in what had caused the code blue. Josef was in his late fifties, and he obviously had a bad heart. She'd noticed minor changes in his EKG after surgery, indicating a possible mild myocardial infarction. The surgeon had ordered serial cardiac enzyme tests to see how much damage his heart had sustained.

Obviously more than they'd realized.

The ruckus didn't settle down for a long while. After she'd given her story to what seemed like dozens of agents, they allowed her to leave. As she gathered her scattered paperwork into some semblance of order, she listened to the ongoing debate.

Some of the problems were simple, like who should talk to the media at the press conference. But others were more difficult, such as who would oversee Josef Korolev's autopsy—someone from the US government or Russian medical examiners? After a heated argument, it was decided both sides would be present during the procedure.

But by the time she was able to leave, a couple of hours after the code blue, she had not seen any of the three men who'd stopped in to visit Josef's room earlier that evening. She'd mentioned it to the agents, and their names were on the guard's infamous list.

Their glaring absence, in the face of Josef's death, gnawed at her on the way home.

Natalia fingered her moon pendant and cross as she rode the red Metro train, grateful for its calming effect. Had she imagined Josef Korolev's odd reaction to her pendant? Had he recognized it, or was it similar to something he'd seen before? Maybe the design, the symbol of a crescent moon with three stars on one end, was specifically Russian in nature. She could easily picture a little shop in Moscow where dozens of pendants just like hers were sold.

She'd concentrated on finding her birth mother through deciphering her adopted mother's journal. She'd never considered the necklace design in itself to be important.

Josef's reaction convinced her that the moon-shaped pendant was a clue. Her chest swelled with anticipation at the thought. She knew her birth mother was Russian, as her adopted mother was. Other than the first name of Anya, she didn't know anything else about her birth mother. Since her adopted mother had passed away three years ago, she'd intensified her search for her roots. Had become obsessed with knowing who she was and who the woman was who'd given her away. Natalia had collected as much information as she could about Kazan, the city of her birth.

As soon as she got home, she'd add this new puzzle piece to the other bits of information she'd gathered about her birth mother. Maybe researching the pendant on the internet would reveal something she'd missed.

A young man shuffled past her, pressing purposefully against her. She dodged him, slipped a hand into her canvas bag, and closed her fingers around the can of pepper spray hidden in there. The crime rate was notorious in DC, and she was jittery enough after the strange events during her shift.

The guy took a seat across from her on the other side of the train. She took a deep breath, then let it out slowly, but she didn't relax her grip on the pepper spray. Illegal or not, she intended to use the weapon if needed.

Ignoring the man staring at her, she trained her gaze on a spider web in the corner of the car. A fly caught in the silken strands fought to get free.

A shiver rippled along her nerves, and she glanced away. Anxious, she waited for her stop to come up. She wanted nothing more than to get home.

Stepping off the train at her Brookland stop, she hurried up the stairs to the main level, staring straight ahead but screening the people around her from the corner of her eye. The events at the hospital had put her on edge. For a moment, she thought the man coming up on her left side looked familiar, but then he turned and headed off in the opposite direction.

Ridiculous to be so paranoid. She gave herself a mental shake. She was a critical care nurse. It wasn't as if she were the one in danger.

Not like Josef Korolev had been. Someone hated him or what he represented enough to shoot him. To ultimately cause his death. Although the Cold War had been declared over decades ago, the animosity between Russia and the US hadn't changed much. If a member of the Russian Mafia was the killer, why wait until Josef was on US soil to finish him off?

Nothing made sense.

She used her rideshare app to get a ride. It didn't take long for a guy in a black sedan to drive up next to her. "Are you Natalia?"

"Yes, thanks." Her house was only a dozen

blocks from the Metro station, but she didn't care. She'd pay him extra for his time. "My address is eleven forty-one Girard Street."

The driver grunted, shrugged, and pulled into traffic. Natalia dropped her head against the back of the seat. Thankfully, she was almost home. She considered having a dish of ice cream to relax after her wretched day. At least tomorrow was Friday and she had the weekend off.

"Here ya go, lady."

She opened her eyes, realizing the rideshare had pulled over to the curb. He'd stopped in front of the house next to hers, but she wasn't in the mood to argue.

"Thank you." She added a tip to the rideshare fare via the app on her phone, then opened the door, swung her legs out, gathered her canvas bag, and stood.

Ka-boom! The blast rocked the stillness of the night. The ground trembled beneath her feet. She stumbled and fell backward into the sedan.

The windows burst outward in a hailstorm of glass. Shards rained down against the car like bullets from a machine gun as a second explosion shattered the night.

It took her a moment to realize it was her house, the precious home she had once shared with her mother, engulfed in roaring flames.

www.ingramcontent.com/pod-product-compliance
Lightning Source LLC
Chambersburg PA
CBHW071811190726
48292CB00008B/2796

9781949144505